T0142733

Life of a Thai Masseuse

Life of a Thai Masseuse

The Beginning

Natesan Sarvanam

PARTRIDGE

A Penguin Random House Company

ISBN: Hardcover   978-1-4828-7135-7
            Softcover   978-1-4828-7134-0
            eBook   978-1-4828-7136-4

To order additional copies of this book, contact
Partridge India
000 800 10062 62
orders.india@partridgepublishing.com

www.partridgepublishing.com/india

In all my travels, I have gained great insights into many cultures and traditions. I am fascinated by the Thai people and their down-to-earth attitude. My innumerable visits to Thailand for the last ten years have made me feel like a different human being compared to the run-of-the-mill urban male. The honesty, beauty, and straightforwardness of the village folks along with their tasty food are a delight.

I have spent a lot of time talking to people in Bangkok, Pattaya, Krabi, Phi Phi Island, Koh Samui, and Phuket to understand their feelings on life and its intricacies. Most of them believe in Lord Buddha to take care of them. They revere and worship the king, queen, and the royal family to protect them for all time to come. The hard work to make money to nurture their families is their prime concern. On a fatalistic note, they believe in karma, destiny, and the will of Buddha. 'Whatever happens in one's life is for one's own good' is their maxim.

I dedicate this novel to the brave, beautiful, and honest humans of Thailand, especially to the people of Issan, the north-eastern part of Thailand.

Acknowledgements

In my journey of life, I have experienced a lot of joys, sorrows, and the power of unknown hands. I have accepted the flow of nectar as a gift, the bitter pills as grace. I am grateful to the universe for keeping me on the 'butter side' of life. My heart bleeds for those in a horrific situation without a slice of bread. The reasons are unfathomable to us, or are they within us yet unknown to us?

I would like to address this issue in my own minuscule way with you, my readers. A good amount of money from this book will help in feeding and educating the needy children of Thailand and India.

I have a friend, philosopher, and guide in my son Praveen Kumar S., who has given his time, knowledge, and wise counsel in writing many of my books, and this book is my maiden publication.

My son advised me to speak my heart out and record the same for it to be transcribed, and I took the cue. I am thankful for the help of Olivia, Moses, and Lauren in transcribing my recordings to my satisfaction. I appreciate the industrious publishing consultants—Marco Bale, Racel Cruz, Pohar Baruah, Antoniet Saints, Marie Giles—and the entire team at Partridge Publishing.

My only believer in my ability and my financial supporter, who stood by me, is a great human being, Mr Manjunath Pai, a successful hotelier from Mumbai, India.

Last but not the least, I am grateful to my family and friends for their continued love, affection, and support.

Chapter 1

My name is Mai. I hail from a village which is located near Sisaket in Issan, the north-eastern part of Thailand. I had a very cooperative childhood. I'll explain later the meaning of *cooperative childhood*. It was a small village where there were two hundred to three hundred houses and five hundred to six hundred people living in it. There was a temple of Buddha, which is called a *wat* in the Thai language. I'm a Buddhist by practice and by birth. Like all children, I was also told what was good, what was bad, what was ugly. I didn't understand the meaning of *bad* and *ugly*. I knew only *good*.

All the houses, which were next to one another and across and nearby, had neat roads and small gardens. Majority of the houses were built of wood; only a few houses were built with brick and mortar, those for the rich. The people were loving. Anybody could walk into anybody's house any time without knocking and talk to them. The neighbour three doors away could speak to the other person on the other side of the street in a loud voice. Everybody used to interfere in one another's affairs. For any problem in a family, everybody used to get involved, talking, shouting, and gesticulating.

You may not know it, but the Thai language is a tonal language. It is very sing-song, beautiful, and a lot of expressions are thrown in when you speak. Exclamations, questions, sadness, happiness—all is shown through the way you speak to the other person; half of the job is done. It's not a plain language wherein you control your emotions and try to convey your feelings to the other person. It is different in Thailand. People are just spontaneous and pour their hearts out. Ten people talk at the same time about the same topic, and everybody understands whatever is said. It's awesome. You can never know how they manage to speak with one another.

So my cooperative childhood was vibrant. We used to eat anybody's food—no grace said, no dining table set, no five-course dinners. It was just the basics. The rice was the staple food, and a watery curry, soup, and sometimes fish, crabs, prawns, seafood, noodles, or all kinds of vegetables were thrown in. Though just two times a day—one in the morning at nine o'clock, ten o'clock, and again in the evening at five o'clock, six o'clock, or seven o'clock—we enjoyed the simple food.

There was not much fancy in what we ate, and not much of oil was used for frying. Yes, it was there, but basically, everything was a very simple affair. Spicy food with lots of ginger, galangal, lime, garlic, chillies, basil and few other herbs, spices, and condiments thrown in and a lot of greens, spinach added—it was a very balanced food as far as health was concerned. There is less fat content in most of the food of Thais, but of course, the passion of Thailand is pork, and we all love it though it is very expensive.

We went down to the fields, all the kids, to catch a lot of small flying grasshoppers and so many other insects. All collected them, and believe me, they were nicely fried and eaten. You may call us pagans. Yes, we are all pagans. We have risen from this earth—ashes to ashes, dust to dust—to enjoy the bounties of Mother Earth. We all go back to the originating point after we complete our task in this world.

Well, we started to produce rice two times in a year, depending on the god of rain. Everybody had a garden, and we all shared the produce with all our neighbours. Thais have the rain god or the water god, and then we have the fire god, the god of air, and the god of space. We revere Mother Earth as our living god. We see the dance of the paddy crops as the dance of Mother Earth in ecstasy to fill our bellies. Whatever you eat has a bit of earth in it. You may wash it before you cook, but a small portion will get into your system. It's good for your health—absolutely no harm done.

Now going back to this cooperative childhood, I grew up beautifully in my own way, playing with boys and girls with great abandon. Everyone fought with everyone. The Oedipus complex worked—boys attracted to girls, girls attracted to boys. A man is attracted to a woman, and a woman is attracted to a man, and always, the opposites work. For good, there is bad; for night, there is day. When you have nothing, you want something; the greed factor never allows you to be satisfied.

So in our cooperative childhood, we developed traits of hard work, eagerness to work, eagerness to eat, eagerness to play, and eagerness to enjoy. The concept of having a temple or a wat is that it functions more or less like a community centre, where all the people can congregate and share their chit-chats like any other get-together. We had many feasts in memory of dead priests, living priests, and future priests. In these feasts, a lot of food was served. That was what we children wanted—lots of rice, ice-cool drinks, coffee, pork, seafood, chicken, and vegetables. What more could we want?

That was how life went on; we were taught a few chants or mantras to invoke the blessings of the lord almighty. It is like the Bible being read and the priest explaining the content in a simpler language; you may understand the meaning of what the priest says and try to relate it to your life to know what the future holds for you. Similarly, we chant and understand from the holy books of Buddhism, and we listen to the holy words from the monks for our well being.

Life went on with so much happiness. The rich and the poor children, the boys and the girls—all mingled together. There was no difference between haves and have-nots. All were treated equally. I think by the age of seven, I was trained, told, and made to understand the higher strata of people and the lower strata of people and that I was in the middle. I was told that a particular boy or girl was a rich man's child, that they had a lot of money, and that I had to respect them. I had to be careful with them.

But until we were seven, we used to fight, hit one another, and played together, and it was all one big merry-go-round. I was told that when I reached the age of seven, my life would change. The lines in my palm would change once in seven years, and my destiny would be rewritten. Similarly, in my life at the age of seven, I was brainwashed, totally told to differentiate between people to people. I was unable to understand why, for seven years, there had been no difference and why, when I was seven, I was supposed to be careful and to give more respect to one person but could treat another person carelessly because that person was lower than my level.

See the hierarchy inculcation done by the society. Now, I am able to analyze all this, but at the age of seven, I used to brush off all that my mama and papa used to say, and we used to go and play. Likewise, the other children, whether from the lower or upper ranks, never bothered. We used to go chase a lot of pigs, cows. We used to take a ride on buffaloes.

It was great fun. There were races organized where we could sit on a buffalo and others sat on other buffaloes and we would try to ride on them and finish first in the race. Life was one celebration, but once we reached eight years, nine years, we were told to be more diligent, to be more responsible. The burden of poverty got into our bones.

I've been told by a European that they have the basics; they're not too bothered about their food, shelter, clothing, and all other needed things. They are available and taken care of by family, parents, and the government. We do have a welfare system in Thailand for senior citizens and handicapped people and have health schemes for the poor. But the affluence of the West is not there in Asian countries.

As we grew up, we thought that maybe the gods were not very happy with us and whether we were the children of lesser gods. But everybody is equal in the eyes of our god; only the greed, the selfishness, the utter apathy towards others by those in power has brought in so many abnormalities in the system of life. Believe me, we in Thailand are very blessed because we have a benevolent king and queen and their family works hard for our well-being. They help us by bringing in new technologies, new systems from all over the world. They strive hard to protect us and take care of us. We have great respect for the royal family, who are our gods next to Buddha.

I became philosophical because I was exposed to various people. I must have met people of many nationalities— Asians, Europeans, Africans, Australians, New Zealanders, and of course, Americans. From all over the world, people come to Thailand. They love our food, our culture. They love us; they like us very much. We are beautiful, pretty, obedient, willing to understand, willing to listen to them.

Most of the guys complain either to a man or a woman that their partner does not listen to them, are too busy, do not respect them, take care of them, or look after them. They feel small sometimes. I remember one guy—maybe he was fifty-five, sixty—telling me that he used to go with a lot of pep, a lot of enthusiasm near his wife. She would tell him, 'What do you want?' He would smile, but she would say, 'What can you do? You cannot perform, you cannot give me happiness. What's the point? Go to sleep!' The poor guy was crestfallen; he had no faith to assert himself because she was telling the truth—he could not get a proper erection. He needed a well-erected organ to please his lady love and give her an orgasm. The lady did not understand that she could manage to get an orgasm with her husband's help through love and patience.

So the weaknesses, pitfalls—all are very natural. Many say that with too much drinking, you lose the libido, your sexual urge; you cannot perform, and you become impotent. This is what is told, I believe, by many doctors to many of my friends. Please remember, when a congenial atmosphere is created, when a sympathetic person listens to your woes and shares your feelings, your confidence will be boosted. You have to develop the positive vibes to give a proper booster to their ego is to be taken care of. A man or woman can both perform, and both can have an orgasm with no issues. It is a matter of understanding, patience, knowing the ropes. No two individuals are made the same, but for every individual, there is a special solution. Humans are all made equal but unequal maybe in terms of money, colour, size, height, weight, situations, good luck, and bad luck. With all said and done, the power, existence, and godliness has been created equal in everybody. Everybody has a body; everybody has all the organs. Maybe a few unlucky ones are missing a few things, but the majority has everything. Each one will work properly in a congenial atmosphere.

People say 'Some are smart, some are very good' or 'He picked up everything very fast'. Two children may be from the same parents, same school, same background, but both are different. Why that difference? No one knows. There is plenty of money spent on a lot of experiments by scientists to understand everything. But there is no money spent or experiments done to understand human beings, their feelings, their needs, their fears, their anxieties, and their futile search for happiness. They are all missing. There is not a single experiment done on how to make a person happy. Have we found out or produced a person who can be happy all the time or one, who can be unhappy all the time? No, life is full of ups and downs. We have to adjust accordingly. There is an unknown power which is guiding all our lives.

Chapter 2

One fine day, I started bleeding in my private part, the vagina. I was scared. Mama told me not to worry, and I was taken care of and initiated into the process of understanding the menstrual cycle of twenty-eight days; whatever number of days of high and low was explained to me. I was told to be careful and to mingle with boys in a very, very careful way. In our society, the ordinary folks do not have the overall knowledge to protect themselves, whereas the educated ones with their knowledge and financial power take care of themselves.

In Thailand, a girl who reaches puberty gets preferential treatment. She is given nutritious food and lots of rest for her to adjust to the changes the menstrual cycle brings in. Her relatives and friends are informed and invited to the house to bless the girl for her great future. A great future simply means finding a good husband. It is an advertisement or announcement: 'My girl is fertile and can bear many children. You are welcome to choose her as your wife.' The girl child is considered as a symbol of fertility as fertile as Mother Earth. The girl child brings in a lot of luck to the family and the community. In Thailand, the lady is the boss of the house; she gets preference over others in family functions. In many other Asian cultures, it is the other way round. The parents do not want a girl because they have to pay a huge dowry and meet marriage expenses. There are plenty of cases wherein they abort a female foetus after they come to know the baby's gender through scanning.

The affluent children have the guidance of their educated parents, and they understand the words *hygiene* and *menstrual cycle*, and at the same time, they're taught about it in school when they go to higher standards. All this is possible because they have better financial strength. In my case, I was going to a village school with the same mind-set as the local villagers, so everything was done in a hush-hush manner, like in other Asian countries.

I understood that I had an advantage in being a girl as I was pretty, and I understood the disadvantage of being a girl that I was the target of boys for their jokes. Of course, I did have a liking, but I was told it was not very good; I was supposed to protect myself. Many friends explained to me that it was safe to be away from the boys. I was attracted to boys in my mind. The fantasies, the feelings, the changes in my body were the catalyst. The forbidden fruit is always tastier, but it is safer to maintain distance.

Generally, in Asia it is always the parents of a boy and a girl who fix marriages according to their social status, caste, and religion. The trend is slowly changing as the girls are encouraged to work, and in the process, they meet many guys; they do fall in love.

Thailand follows the matriarchal system. The boy who marries the girl will have to go to live in the girl's house. The boy is supposed to give a dowry to the bride. It's nice to know that for a change, the girl is respected. In other Asian cultures, the girl is supposed to give a dowry to the boy, and the girl goes to live in the boy's house; that is the patriarchal system.

I, for one, didn't know anything about all these things. Being a young girl learning the Thai language, I used to bunk my English classes. Only one class a week, and I was not interested. I used to go and chit-chat or play with my other friends because English was not very lovable at that time. Now I regret that I had not learned English. The result is, I have broken English. I am now trying to learn more English since that's the universal language as of today if you want to go anywhere in the world.

I got married to a handsome boy when I was eighteen, and he was twenty-two years old. He was a good guy, and they gave me a good dowry by Thai standards. The boy started to live with me in my house. Life was excellent—good food, good husband, good family, good neighbours. We celebrated many festivals like Songkran (that's the celebration for the new year) and many other festivals of Thailand—Spring Festival, sowing festival, temple festival, and so on and so forth. My husband was very hard-working and industrious.

A wedding in Thailand is a very fun-filled, interesting, and exciting event, especially in a village. The whole village and its residents are totally involved in the preparation for the marriage. The inner circle—that is, the relatives and close friends—is totally immersed in preparing for the wedding and the wedding feast. They'll forget all their work, all their worries, and all their problems and dive deep into the wedding preparations of that particular person in the village.

I was no exception. I was loved, liked, and appreciated for my cooperative behaviour, and my willingness to adjust with the people had earned me lots of friends. The people from the boy's house came. We all received the boy and his family, friends, and relatives and accommodated them. There was no fancy accommodation involved; anybody could sleep anywhere. On the floor, a mat is spread. If there was no pillow, the hand became the pillow, and everybody slept at twelve o'clock, one o'clock, or two o'clock in the night. Of course, the celebration involves good food and alcohol, so you'll sleep more deeply. It's a temporary phenomenon, but it helps in sleeping. Even if the mosquitoes bite you, you will not know.

I was excited in my heart. There were many tales of how the boy was offered many girls; girls from richer families all wanted to marry him, him being a handsome man, but he chose me for my beauty. You know, my ego shot up. I felt thrilled, I felt nice, and my body was quaking with the anticipation of getting married. I didn't know much, but I had a fair idea of what it meant. I've seen many weddings down in the village.

The D-day came. A lot of food was prepared—prawns, fish, pork, duck, chicken. In our village, most of us didn't consume beef or lamb meat. When everything was ready, the priest came, and the elaborate ritual took place. In Thailand, normally a thread is tied around the hands of the girl and the boy together, and the thread goes through the priest to Buddha. There is a lot of religious significance to all this, and of course, it suffices to say that the two people are united for eternity.

There was a vow-taking ceremony, and we pledged our allegiance to each other till death parted us. I was told that whether it's Christianity, Islam, Hinduism, or any other religion, the bond is built to facilitate the union of two people. At the ceremony, we were served hard liquor to be consumed by us. A little sip was taken, the head of a pig was kept on a big plate, two candles were burning on the side, and on a big banana leaf, betel leaves, betel nuts, fruits, and flowers were all kept with sixty thousand baht in cash (that is two thousand US dollars) as the dowry money to the bride.

As soon as the wedding ritual was completed, everybody was served with liquor, rice, and all the delicacies prepared for the wedding. Everybody helped themselves, and all were very pleased and happy. And the wedding was finished, simple and straightforward.

Of course, in a city, it's more elaborate. Marriages are done in big halls, and many guests come in. Many other rituals are added depending on how rich you are. Loud recorded music is played, and it is played throughout the night. Everybody drinks; everybody dances. The ones with lots of money will organize bands, music parties, and five girls, ten girls, or fifteen girls will perform for two to three hours.

Leading the guests, the bride and the groom also join their friends and dance to the tempo of the music. They all dance, drink, and forget the whole world. It's a celebration time. Then, I thought, deep down in ancient civilization, dance must have been an integral part in all societies. The body works, and the chemicals all mix up and give a lot of acceleration, a lot of happiness. You enjoy and your mind is relaxed and you're in a mood to be very happy. This, I suppose, is heaven, the correct seventh heaven. As far as I know, nobody has seen heaven. I suppose this is heaven.

After the wedding ceremony was over, I was drowsy. I was slightly drunk with the bit of alcohol taken. The boy, my husband, was also a little drunk. But I could see the fire in his eyes. I could see his lust. He was eager and waiting to touch me, to feel me, to take me. I understood 50 per cent of it, maybe a little more, but I didn't know exactly how it would be because I had no experience. Anything comes by practice. My husband and I, were sent into the room. He received me; he started talking. Outside the room, music played on.

People around were singing, shouting. Many were drunk, fighting, laughing; it was total peace and chaos. The whole place was full of sound.

He first held me. I was shivering. My whole body was shaking, but I was also certain there was no air con working but only a fan. He hugged me, he kissed me, and he started touching me. It was a new experience; my whole body was under fireworks. I had the feeling that my breasts were swelling. My loins were churning, and my vagina was getting wet—great new achievements. He was hugging me and kissing me all over my body. We both were looking at each other with so much love and affection. He went behind me and started kissing my neck. Both his hands were busy on my breasts, and his erect penis was moving on my buttocks. I felt great, and my whole body was trembling with pleasure. I was glued to him. We both were merged into a single body. My head was bursting. I was wondering what was happening to me. Slowly, I could feel his bulge. I could feel his penis rubbing against me. I was surprised. It was a long one by Asian standards.

In Asia generally, the penis of a man is not very long or short, but when excited, it can be a full five inches, maybe more or less depending on one's race. I was told by expert customers that what matters is two and a half inches; again, it is the thickness that makes all the difference in giving your best to your partner.

I didn't know about my husband's; I hadn't measured. But it was hard, and he was rubbing me all over my body. He slowly undressed me. My small breasts were swollen; I'd not seen them become so big. When I showered and applied soap, they would become a little big, and my nipples would become a little hard. But now, it was totally swollen, and I was breathing hoarsely. He started rubbing them, he started fondling them, and slowly, he started sucking them. The feeling was totally new, exciting, unique, and out of this world.

I understood slowly so much of happiness, so much of the feelings a touch of a man on a woman can produce. I had not felt it when I touched myself. The magic was on. He started sucking my breasts.

I was moaning. I was uttering words, and he said, 'Slow down. Control your emotions. People are outside. Maybe many are waiting to listen to odd sounds from our room. We have no privacy, especially today.'

There were lots of guests. I tried to control myself, but I couldn't. He was also sounding hoarse; he seemed to know a bit of the ropes of having sex. I dared not ask him whether he had had any previous experience, but he did ask me, and I said that this was my first time. He started sucking my breasts; I had a rumbling in my vagina. I felt the wetness coming from there. Some water was dripping down from my vagina, and I mistook it for urine. I didn't know the difference between the urinary and vaginal tracts. I had no knowledge of my body parts and their reactions to this situation (though now I know all the parts, their functions, and their reactions).

He started slowly touching me, rubbing me, and he suggested that I should part my legs, which I did. He slowly removed his clothes. When I felt his manhood, which was put in my hand, I was so excited—the strong, hard, muscled penis. He asked me to fondle it, touch it. He was touching me all over my vaginal area, then he couldn't hold on to it. He was totally excited. He slowly, steadily opened me up and entered me. It was very painful. I started crying.

He said, 'Don't cry. The first time is always painful. You will be fine.'

It's normal in Asia that on the first night of the wedding of a boy and a girl, a white bed sheet is spread on the mattress. The next day, someone from the boy's family, either the mother or sister, goes and sees whether there are any blood marks on the bed sheets. I suppose, it's the proof of the virginity of a girl.

I was moaning in pain. He slowly and steadily entered my vagina. I was between heaven and hell. It was very, very painful, but at the same time it was very pleasurable. I felt terrible, and at the same time, I felt it was very nice. After some time, he slowly moved.

I said, 'Slow down. It's painful.'

He said, 'Relax, you will be fine.'

Then he thrust four or five times, I don't remember. Then there was an explosion. I had a great orgasm. Water was pouring from my vagina, and he exploded. His semen was all over the inside of my body. I was totally taken away by this experience. Was this what marriage was all about? Was this all of heaven and earth working? Was this the second hunger?

The first hunger, of course, is food. If you don't eat when you are hungry, you cannot have the strength to do anything. You need the strength; you need food. Once your stomach is full, the thought of sex comes in. That is the second hunger. That was how the second hunger was introduced to me.

A little later, I felt the withdrawal of his penis from my vagina, and I felt the hot liquid—that is, his semen—pouring out of my body. He gave me a towel to clean myself with. There was no attached bathroom; I had to go out if I wanted to use the bathroom. I was scared. He cleaned himself, then he dressed. He then hugged me and kissed me, and then he went to sleep on his side of the bed. I followed suit. I wanted to go and clean myself. I was feeling dirty. There was blood on my body, on the bed sheet. I wanted to, but he said, 'Sleep, and tomorrow morning, you can do all that.' He had one more shot of the liquor that was there; he offered it to me, and I took a sip, maybe more. We slept like a log. I did not get up in the middle of the night till I was disturbed. My married life started like that.

Somewhere around four o'clock in the morning, he got up. He woke me up, and he went through the same ritual again. He fondled my breasts, kept on sucking them for a long time. This in turn gave me a great kick. I was moaning loudly, unleashing my passions. He asked me to control myself and just enjoy it. My whole body was vibrating in anticipation of his penis entering my vagina. This time, it was easier, and it lasted longer than the first time. He asked me to put both my legs around his buttocks so that the penetration would be deeper. He kept on pumping vigorously as his penis grew in size. I was also building up and matched his every stroke. We both reached the crescendo with a great burst of semen and my cum. He was mighty happy—me too. I also enjoyed it.

We slept until morning. Maybe we got up around six o'clock. There was a knock on my door, and I hurriedly went and opened the door. My mother asked me to go out, to take a shower, and to wash myself. I rushed. Then the boy's mother and sister came, and they saw the stains and the blood marks on the bed sheet. They looked at the boy. He nodded, and they felt all was fine. They were very, very pleased they got a virgin bride.

But where is the test, where are the blood marks for the boy to prove he is a virgin? Look at the partiality; look at nature and maker's lopsided views on the situation. Why has the god not given that kind of scenario or that kind of situation to men? So that's the reason, from time immemorial, men have puffed egos and feelings of omnipotence. There are many disadvantages to being a woman, and this is one of them. You have to prove your virginity, especially in Asia. Do you know? I have read that many girls from affluent families go to a doctor, a surgeon, and get their hymen reconstructed before their weddings. Either they have lost it to their boyfriends or in any other manner of self-gratification. They get it reconstructed—the hymen—so that on the first night, the husband will have the pleasure of getting a virgin. Look at how selfish the men are and how smart the modern girls are!

The next day, the feast continued; it went on for at least three days. One day before the wedding and one day after the wedding, the boy and the girl—that's me and my husband—both fell at the feet of all elders, took their blessings, and our life started on that note. We had no concept of honeymoon; honeymoons were only for the rich. We had our honeymoon in our houses. That was how my life with my husband started.

In my case, my life was blissful. We were working in the field together, rubbing each other while putting seeds into the land. We would have mud in our hands while we fixed the paddy plants at correct intervals. We were having a good time, a very happy life. Early in the morning, we would rush to the field by five o'clock in the morning after drinking rice mixed in water or rice and some leftover soup from the night before. We'd go work in the field, come back by 10 a.m., and hot food would be ready, rice and some fish, which was expensive but a delicacy. We used to get fish, prawns, pork, which was our staple diet. Of course, we used to collect a lot of insects that would fly around, fry them nicely, and eat them heartily. Maybe, it is difficult for people to understand our eating habits, but that was how we had been eating since our childhood.

We used to go on some pretext to my room and have sex. Sometimes we would stop halfway and go back outside because my mama and papa would shout, 'Where the hell are you guys?' We would go back running, half-satisfied. Sometimes we would finish it fast and have a great orgasm. We would go back to the field and work, and he would give me that kind of look that he was totally satisfied. There was a lot of love in his eyes, and he would always steal a kiss. Sometimes my dad or mom would look at it and shout at him, 'Go and do the work! Do not look at your beautiful wife!' I would smile. I was pleased. I was in seventh heaven. I thought this life was beautiful, enjoyable, and great! I was the most beautiful girl in the world. I used to put a lot of talcum powder, which was the make-up material of a village girl. I loved and cherished those beautiful days. Now, I am forty-three, and I am full of make-up to attract my customers.

While I worked, there would suddenly be a burst of wetness in my vagina. I used to wonder what it was. The semen would drip from my thighs. I was happy, and I took care of it. That was how I enjoyed my sexual life; I felt it was great. After my hunger for food, my hunger for my husband's body was predominant by six in the evening. After we finished working in the field, we would go back home, wash, help my mother in cooking whatever dishes she was making, which were sometimes nicely fried fish, pork, and rice. We rarely consumed sweets; sugar was taboo. That was the reason we were all thin, beautiful. Our complexions were lovely; maybe it was because of the tropical climate. We were in the sun, so we got free vitamins.

In a newly married household, there is a lot of liquor available; generally, all men and women drink after a hard day's work in Thailand. But I was not interested in drinks. I was not keen. If someone forced me, I would take a little, but my husband drank regularly. Then we would go to bed around eight o'clock in the night; that was the maximum. We would chit-chat a little after eating. Whether it was with friends, neighbours, or visitors, we'd talk, talk, talk. 'Bak, bak, bak' is what they say in Thailand. Then we would go to bed. I used to be eager for sex. I had a great appetite, always enjoying it. But after the first month, our two times, three times in a day turned into one time. After two to three months, we only did it every other day and, after six months to one year, twice a week. That became the standard rule.

Chapter 3

Later on, as I was in the massage business, I met many, many Europeans, Westerners, Americans, Asians. I was told that if you drink liquor too much every day (three, four, five pegs), you lose interest in sex. Alcohol reduces the appetite for sex—this is what most of them told me. I am not a scientist, so I have no proof, but this is what I was told. Maybe it is true because my husband became a 'twice a week' man. I used to sometimes grope him, encourage him, and three times might be possible if he was excited. But he started slowly losing interest in sex. I was ever ready, but it can be said that he was never ready.

I became pregnant. Pregnancy put me at a disadvantage from the sex point, but on the emotional point, I was very happy. I was going to become a mother! Almost all women in this world enjoy motherhood. The modern mother might not like it, but mostly, everyone enjoys motherhood because the bodily changes, the emotional changes, the child's movements, and the sudden kick of the child from the stomach—all that is so exciting! In Asia, the normal citizens do not know the exact details of how a child is formed, how you should conduct yourself, how you should protect the child, when you should abstain from sex, the first three months, the crucial period, all the injections you are supposed to take to protect yourself and the child.

We did not know anything. When I was pregnant, I continued to work, to have sex. Frequency was reduced as my stomach grew. My husband was not interested because his two times a week became one time a week. I had nausea, and I vomited in the beginning. Later on, my bulge did not allow me to have aggressive or active sex. We did not know the postures to be adopted. Necessity is the mother of invention. We used to adopt side postures. The man has only one aim; he wants to pour out his semen. Once that is done, he is finished, whereas it takes time for a woman to achieve her orgasm. She needs to become hot, but that's not taken care of by the man. He's only interested in himself. Drunk he comes, finishes in a few minutes, and goes away. What will a woman do? She is just ready; she has to be frustrated.

I was getting frustrated, but the compensation was my child in my stomach. The time would come after nine months and nine days and nine hours and nine minutes and nine seconds—the time taken, the elders claimed, for delivering a child.

I was a hard-working woman. I worked in the field even in the ninth month—lighter jobs because I couldn't bend much. But I used to do other jobs. I used to help my mom with the cooking. I used to clean the house, wash clothes (of course, now I have a washing machine). In those days, we used to manually wash our clothes and dishes (no dishwasher then and, even today, still no dishwasher). We had very few dishes, not like in the urban areas where they have many vessels for each item to be cooked. They clean even fifty dishes in a household in the urban areas. But in the village, we had one or two small pans and one or two small aluminium vessels in which to make the soup, fry, and cook the rice.

Now we have rice cookers—what an evolution in these twenty years. Today, in a village in Thailand, you sit right from eight in the morning, and many vehicles will come, selling fish, vegetables, fruits, furniture, utensils, mattresses, all the household things, cement, steel, roofing materials. Name all you need; everything is brought to you at your doorstep and given to you, for which you pay in six or twelve monthly instalments. That is how products are marketed these days.

In Thailand we do not consume milk much and drink very little coffee or tea. Just coffee, it's all black; tea, it's all black. Lactose is a taboo in most households. Maybe it's not so good; it's not required for the body. 'Not easily digestible' is what I think was told to me by the learned ones.

Life became different after my son was born. I looked at him, and I was smiling. He was smiling, and my husband was smiling. My papa, mama, father-in-law, mother-in-law, brothers, cousins, friends, relatives—everybody was smiling. Again, it was a happy celebration, happy eating, happy drinking, happy dancing. It was great; everything was a celebration of joy! Of course, everything required money, but in our way of life, we did not care. We sold things, borrowed money on interest, and we celebrated! We hoped the rain would come, crops would grow, grain would come, rice would be sold, money would come, and we could clear the loan—and again, borrow. It's a cycle, a curse on the farmers of Asia, who depend on the mercy of the weather god.

That is the reason we worship nature. We were all pagans until Buddhism was introduced to us. We have hung on to Buddha, fervent prayers being given to him to give us all the bounties of nature. We are very blessed. We do have water, rain, greenery; all is given by Mother Nature. We are a blessed country in our own right, and we enjoy it. We have a great king and queen, who takes care of all of us and whom we revere as next to Buddha or as Buddha. Long live the king and the queen and the royal family.

My son started growing. I used to breastfeed him now that plenty of milk was available. I used to force him to have some, and sometimes I would be in pain because he was not drinking sufficient milk. One more thing you should know; any lady with a small child can offer her excess milk to another child in the village. For example, let's assume that in the village, five or ten girls have given birth to children. Some don't have milk, some have little milk, and some have more than needed. The children are brought in for the community sharing of the milk. Even at midnight, if a child cries of hunger, you can bring the child to the mother with more milk and feed the child. That is the concept of community living in a village in Thailand. What a great thing!

I was told it's unheard of in a Western country. All Europeans, all the oldies, or all the young ones who come to Thailand have many tales to tell us on the disparities between the East and the West. I was told by my friend that Mark Twain said the East and West will never meet. Maybe on a few points he is right. Believe me, only in Thailand and Cambodia can a ninety-year-old man hold an eighteen-year-old girl's hand or maybe two girls or three girls even if he is in a wheelchair. One girl can hold his hand, and the two girls put him in a wheelchair and take him on a stroll on the beach; nobody will question it. That is the power of money, sharing and exchanging of one another's resources to meet one another's needs.

That's how it is. A sixty- or seventy-year-old guy can hold a twenty-year-old lady's hand and go walking, both smiling and both chit chatting whether she understands his language or not. He may not also understand what she is saying, but both are smiling. This is a universal language. They have a lot of love in their eyes. They share each other's needs. Each other's needs are catered to. He has the money; she has the services. A European lady who has all the money and a Thai man who has all the services with him—only in Thailand can this happen, nowhere else.

A good friend of mine, a European, told me that they see in Western countries a lot of girls who are in this line of work—hospitality. They stand in the streets to be taken by guys who arrive in their cars. They are all young, and their caretakers, who are called pimps, are there. If they are not in their stations, do not do their job properly, or even if they go to the toilet, they are reprimanded. They have to get permission to go to the restroom to attend to nature's call. So commercialized, so money-minded.

I am also money-minded, but women in this line of work in Thailand have more freedom. We can say, 'Not today, I am not interested in working,' and go home to our rooms and sleep. Maybe in big cities in Thailand, women in this line of work are also commercialized, but we are treated humanely. We are free to walk into a police station at any time. We are welcomed, respected with folded hands. Though they know we are in the hospitality industry, we are not ill-treated. They know we bring green bucks to the country's economy. We take care of guys who come with so much aspirations, hopes into our country. We are the real ambassadors of our nation, taking care of all these people.

I have diverted; I wanted to share my feelings with you guys. My child grew, my son. When my first child became a little bigger, my second one was on his way. The frequency of our sexual encounters became once a week, maybe sometimes twice a week, not three times, never. Then there was not much of love or affection or attraction in my husband's eyes or in his words. He became a little careless and acted busy. He used to be very eager to be with me all the time, but his eagerness slowly eroded. Maybe it was after the second child's birth all the problems started. That was how everything happened.

What we all call the seven-year itch came into play. Slowly my husband became rebellious. We had many, many, many fights for the silliest of reasons, and slowly he started to drift away from me. In Thailand, a man and a woman both drink socially. It varies from person to person whether to drink from morning to night or only in the morning and night or for the whole day or on alternate days or once a week or once a month. But generally, everybody drinks, smokes, fights, and rejoices. This was what was happening. But the fights slowly started becoming irreversible. My husband would not talk to me for one day, two days, and then many days. He would go away to his parents' home for quite some time.

Maybe now I understand the disadvantages of the matriarchal system. My husband came to live in my family's house, and he worked in the fields of my family's land. He did not have total financial freedom from the produce which he sold and had to bring in money to our home. I had the upper hand because he was in my house, and again, he was at a disadvantage most of the time because my parents supported me obviously.

One fine day, my husband said, 'Sorry, I cannot live with you. I'm going away.'

I was shattered, taken aback. I tried to make him understand that I needed him. I told him, 'I will apologize and not fight with you. I will not demand anything from you. I will not demand more sex. Let's be happy. We have two children. Let's live together for the sake of our children so that our kids are taken care of by us.'

But he was not willing to understand; he had made up his mind.

I heard many rumours that he was seeing another woman. He was interested in another woman, and he was getting ready to go from this village to the urban jungle—that is, Bangkok, the capital of Thailand. All people are attracted to the city life, which offers many, many, many goodies and activities beyond one's dreams.

He was related to me, this guy, my husband. His parents came; my parents, all the relatives, all the neighbours—everybody got together. But then finally, he was adamant in leaving me. It was agreed that if he went away, we would separate, and that would be it. He took all his things, and he left one fine day. To be very honest, I didn't feel so much pain, but I wondered where I failed him. What made him take such a drastic decision to leave me and my children? He had chosen another woman with a daughter. Maybe she was docile and subservient to him? Maybe I was too dominating? Was he not getting enough sex from me? Was it that he feared he could not match me in our sexual activity? There were many questions in my mind but never to be answered.

Men generally are capricious. They are never satisfied with what they have. They look for different body structures and colours. My husband chose a plain-looking woman who was dark in colour. He had chosen me over many other beautiful girls, but now he left me for somebody else. There is a saying by elders that says, 'You may have the most beautiful wife, but you still need a mediocre sidekick.' A very small percentage of women do chase men for variety, but it is very negligible. From olden times, men have used women as commodities, but they have given certain concessions in modern days. The core issue is that men expect women to be obedient to them though the lady also makes money. In the changing world, with the advent of same-sex marriages, the issue has watered down the dominance of men. Men marry men; let their egos fight it out for supremacy. Women marry women; the ladies are safely away from all the men in the world.

Our first night of separation was the worst night of my life. I was with my children, my mama, and lady relatives, who were chatting on the core subject of why he left me. Many were cursing him, 'Deserting a woman will land him in hell!' 'The tears of a woman will finish him off' was another curse. The night was spent in these discussions till dawn. I was blamed by some as I was overbearing and overconfident in letting him loose. I should have used my charms to bind him to me for all time to come. Many suggested I could still make him come to me by using black magic. But when someone's heart is not for me, how can I force him to come back to me? I was so proud that I had such a handsome husband. Now I had no husband and no support, but I had two children, who were my assets. I became fatalistic. Whatever has to happen will happen; no power on this earth can stop it. I went to the temple, prayed to Lord Buddha for a long time, met the monk, and took his blessings. He was kind and encouraged me by saying, 'Whatever Buddha does for you is for your own good.' I took those words in total, and slowly and steadily calmness spread into my heart. I involved myself with full gusto into the routine of taking care of work, children, and parents.

The following nights, I felt the void; the loneliness was unbearable. I had a small child, my second son, whom I was taking care of, and my first son, who was three years old, all huddled together, crying and wanting to know what was next.

I was at a loss. I was a beautiful woman. I was very desirable sexually. Why did he leave me? What was wrong with me? Where did I go wrong? I had no answers to all this. I was wondering whether this was what we all call karma. In Thailand we believe Buddha does everything for the good. Buddha is there to take care of us. Buddha is our saviour. He's our god, so he knows what's best for us.

I started to work mechanically, taking care of my sons and parents. I had two brothers. One was in Bangkok; the other was helping my parents in the land. The brother who was taking care of the land was a total alcohol addict. From morning to night, he was very high. He didn't work. My old parents worked. They were old but were very strong, healthy, hard-working people who were taking care of all our land. Of course, I was also working shoulder to shoulder with them.

Life went on. We all depended on rain for our food. Sometimes we'd have double crops, but many times, we only had one crop a year. The produce was sold, and the money was used for our day-to-day needs. Our day-to-day needs were very high. We needed so many things, like education for the children. Rice was available, but for all other things— vegetables, fruits, oil, sugar, everything—we needed money to buy them.

We also needed pork, chicken, seafood and clothing. There were no other opportunities for getting any money. The brother who was in Bangkok was sending little money, but that was not sufficient. We were taking care of his daughter's schooling and welfare. When there was no work on the fields, my dad would work as a painter. We all used to do odd jobs in the village to produce money to meet our requirements.

I was at a loss on what to do, and then I remembered that before I got married, I was sent for four years to Bangkok to work as a servant in a rich guy's house to take care of their child. I started thinking, *Why should I not go to Bangkok and work in some other rich person's house as a servant?* In this thought process, I was lost in the jungle of life and was worried about other problems like sexual harassment and ill treatment by the bosses. Men are generally greedy for sex, and they will take it in any form it is available.

Chapter 4

My mama had brought me to Bangkok to leave me at the house of a rich man where I was supposed to take care of a small child. I was so amazed. I was so wonderstruck to look at all those tall buildings, look at all those cars, look at all those planes zooming in the sky. So many people were all dressed nicely. Yes, I was travelling in a car. I was feeling great. My bosses had sent a car to the bus station with a driver to pick us up. My mom was also equally excited though she had visited Bangkok many times. Bangkok is a mysterious and beautiful city. I was told it has quite a number of hotels, entertainment centres, and shopping malls. As we travelled, there were many red lights, and the car would stop, people would cross hurriedly, and then the car would move forward when green lights came on. I was enjoying it. What fun! People were disciplined; they were forced to be disciplined. Why were they not gregarious? Why did they not cross when there was a red light? Yes, they would get killed if they tried, so the pedestrians stopped to allow cars to move forward.

I was enjoying it. It was a great feeling to be in such a big city. I went into the house through a huge gate. The security fellow opened it, and we drove down into the huge house; it had a big garden. We got out, and I carried my small bag with my clothing in it. The items were all taken to my quarters along with my mother, and I was told to keep my things at a particular place.

They said, 'You are going to stay here, and you are going to sleep in this particular place.'

I nodded. My mama was very polite, and we were given food. We were very hungry. We had taken a bus for the ten, eleven hours' ride from my village to Bangkok. We ate greedily of the rice and pork, and we were very pleased. Only when you are hungry, you will understand the food will taste very nice, you will enjoy so much. Even if the food is not tasty, you will feel it is very tasty. That is life! After we cleaned ourselves, we were called in. I went along with my mother. The lady and the gentleman of the house were seated. We both prostrated in front of them and stood in front of them with folded hands. They were wearing expensive clothes; they were all glittering.

They told us, 'Your girl should take care of our child, and she will be responsible in being very attentive to whatever our child does. Her only job is to take care of the child.'

I said, 'Yes, I will.' I was cheeky enough to say, 'I have taken care of many children in my village.'

They smiled and said, 'Okay, we know you're a smart girl, but here you have to follow whatever instructions you are given, and you should follow it verbatim.'

I said, 'Yes, master.'

They said okay. To my mother, they said, 'You can take one year's salary for your daughter, and you can go back to the village.'

And Mama said, 'Yes, master.'

Once more, she worshiped them, and I also did it. We touched the ground to salute them. We were in need of money. All humans are made equal to be unequal. My mama left in the evening so she could take the bus back home, another eleven-hour ride. She was happy because she had money with her.

She told me to behave myself. 'It's not our village where you can do what you like as per your whims and fancies. You have a job here. You have to be diligent, and you have to take care of the child carefully. I should not receive any complaints.'

I said, 'Yes, Mama.'

She kissed me, hugged me, said bye, and she was taken to the bus station by the driver—again, a car ride. I volunteered to go with my mama.

The lady boss was smiling, and she said, 'Okay, go with your mom and come back. You will have a good ride in the car.'

So once more, I went in the car, went to the bus depot, bid farewell to my mama, and came back to the house. My routine started the next day. Once a week, whenever the bosses had time, they would take the child for an outing. They were very religious people. I visited the Temple of the Golden Buddha; a golden statue of Buddha is there in the temple. I visited Wat Arun, the temple dedicated to the sun god, a huge one on the bank of the river Chao Phraya. I visited also the Temple of the Emerald Buddha, which is located in the huge compound of the palace of the king whom we all revered and worshipped.

The child was taken to many places like parks, play areas, and along with the child, I had the pleasure of seeing so many beautiful things in Bangkok. All this made me think, *My god, this is the other side of life*. All my childhood, I had never gone anywhere. Look, Bangkok has huge temples, entertainment areas, parks—all nice things. You can take a nice boat ride. I did it with the child because I was the caretaker of the child. I was very proud. We had such a lovely time. The child liked me. The child got used to me. The child was trying to talk, saying a few words. In our four years of association, the child had grown, was walking, and was used to calling my name. I felt I had developed a bond with the child. I used to get some special eats sometimes, whatever was made for the child, not very spicy because the child could not eat spicy food. I had also reached eighteen years of age, and my bodily changes made me understand that I was ready for marriage.

I took time to adjust to my new role as a servant. I was happy to take care of a small child. I had practice in my village, and so it was not a problem. Then here the child was beautiful, a girl. She was well dressed and had nice clothes, good surroundings; everything was neat, clean, spick and span. I was wondering if all people lived like this? Yes, it was Bangkok, the capital of Thailand. All rich and famous people live in this city. I was very happy in the beginning. The lady of the house was good to me. The man was equally good, and I respected them so much as my benefactors. All the servants sat down on the ground, bent, and sometimes moved on their knees to follow whatever instructions were given without questioning the wisdom.

Generally, Thais are taught to obey the elders, and it is more so with the girls. It's a male-dominated society; men have a say in everything. All over Asia, all over the world, whether it is in the East or West, in all countries, men dominate. I was told the ladies of America fought a hard battle to get permission to vote in elections. What a tragedy! But what a triumph for the women! The latest success of women is to vote in Saudi Arabia.

So women as such are always subjugated; it is extreme in Asia and worse in poorer countries, like India, Thailand, Cambodia, Vietnam, South East Asia, and maybe in China. I have not gone there, but I have heard many people live there, a huge country. I was wondering that I was in such a beautiful place, a big palatial bungalow. The lawn reminded me of my village and my small garden. There I used to pluck some fruits grown in my garden and eat them. I was proud to say that I was now taking care of a child. There were many other servants. We were all given a place to sleep. We had our own kitchen. We would get our usual fare of rice and soup or maybe the leftovers of many delicacies after the dinner of the bosses and the household members. We were allowed to eat it; otherwise, it was wasted. It was the same system, I suppose, all over the world, maybe with some differences from country to country.

I was in charge of the kid, the only kid in that house. The child was pampered, the child was adored, and the child was my passport for getting special goodies. My life in the city was phenomenal. I understood that life can be so beautiful and people can be so happy. They can eat every day the best food, wear the best clothes, go in the best of cars. Are they specially blessed by Buddha? Yes, I think so. We accept the divinity or the love, the existence or the power, and the godliness which controls all our lives.

I was very happy to play and take care of such a beautiful child full of life. I used to spend my time happily with the child. As time went by the child became naughty and demanding. I would get tired, and I felt maybe in my dreams somebody was holding me. I was totally immersed in my sleep. I got scared and went and reported to my big boss.

I requested the lady of the house, 'I am scared to sleep alone. Will I be permitted to sleep on the ground next to the cot of the child, where the other servant, the older lady who takes care of the child, also sleeps along with the child?'

The boss looked at me. I felt that maybe she was a nice and compassionate lady. She was from a very rich family, a well-known family in Bangkok. She said, 'Okay, you can sleep in the child's room,'

I was overjoyed. I felt all happy and safe. The senior servant lady was also from another village near my village, from Sisaket in the north-east of Thailand. It has a lot of greenery, and the people there are very friendly. This lady told me not to worry, and she took care of me. I was safe in that house.

I had almost completed four years of service with that family, and I had also reached the age of eighteen. The experience, training, and neatness gained in this house helped me to be a better lady in my life. A relative of theirs came to stay with them. He was an old man of forty-five or maybe fifty, I don't know. I think he was fascinated by me.

He was looking at me and asked me, 'Where are you from?' How old are you? You are a beautiful girl.'

I told him, 'Master, I am eighteen years old from a village near Sisaket in Issan.' He would pat me, and he would try to hold me, but I told him, 'Sorry, master.'

I would bend and sit down. He would ask me to massage his legs because he was an old man, and he was in pain. No servant should refuse to massage if the boss's family member wanted it. I was a healthy and strong girl. I did massage him many times, and he was very happy.

They sent word for my family to come down. My mama came in a hurry and met them. She was scared and asked them, 'Did my daughter do anything wrong? Is there a problem?'

They said, 'No, no, no.'

This guy said, 'I will marry your daughter. I'll give you a huge amount as dowry so that you can be very happy in your village. You can repair your house, buy land, and your family will be rich. I will become your son-in-law.'

My mom was overjoyed. She offered to sell me. I use the word *sell*. I'm not a commodity. I cannot be sold. I have a free will. I am a human, not a slave to be sold to somebody just like that, like it happened in the olden days. We all have our own democracy, whatever the meaning of that is. Yes, we are free in Thailand.

So I told my mama, 'I can never marry that guy. Can you not see? He's an old fellow, and he's a wicked guy. He's trying to take advantage of me. I cannot marry him.'

My mama said, 'Look, he gives us big money. You will be a rich lady. You can visit us. Your papa will be a rich man in our village.'

She knew I loved my papa very much. I had the greatest respect for my father, such a nice guy. He was quite hard-working, so lovable. In spite of my protestations, she tried to negotiate the price—maybe for a higher price, I don't know. I said no. I was crying loudly.

The house lady and everybody said, 'Okay, okay. You need not marry him. You can go back to your village.'

So that was it. I escaped the clutches of that rich old man, and I gave myself to a handsome man who deserted me and went away to another woman. What do you call this, fate? Did I write the script of my life? Can I change anything from this? Do I have the liberty to do anything? We in Asia call this as our fate or karma. There are three types of fate. The first is one you bring along with you when you are born, the second one is your accumulated karma from your past lives, and the third is the one you acquire on day-to-day basis. The cumulative effect of all these three karmas will unfold as the real drama of your life. The learned forefathers of many Asian beliefs say so.

My only regret after the episode with that old man who wanted to marry me was leaving the child to whom I got attached; it took me some time to recover from it. I controlled my tears while saying bye to the child, and the child was in tears. She could understand that she would be missing me. They said that if I changed my mind, I could always go back, but I did not go back. That was it.

Chapter 5

The need of the family was so great that we were all wondering, watching all other families in the village. At least one or two members of most of their families were working in big cities some sixty kilometres away, going and coming back every day to their homes. Many were totally moving away to Bangkok or some other big city. That's where the tourists go; that's where the money is.

Thailand's turning point was the Vietnam War. Thailand became the stop point for all American soldiers for rest and relaxation and a good time, and they'd go to fight the Vietnam War. The tourists among us meant money flowed into the bars and the hospitality industry. It was great, and all the money-needing village folks were slowly flocking into the cities to cater to the needs of the tourists; in turn, the money would take care of their children and their families.

In today's world, nobody will give a single dollar to anybody. Maybe they will give one dollar out of sympathy or out of their own mental psyche to a person who begs for that money with the hand of a small child which is twisted, has no leg, or is disfigured. I remember having read of an author of repute saying that he doesn't want to visit Asia, where there is so much of poverty. He's a great man who makes a lot of money with his novels, which are made into hit movies, and although he's one man, he's not willing to see the suffering. What's biting his conscience? I cannot understand. I think pain and pleasure, suffering and happiness are two faces of the same coin.

I was a lady with two children, a father, a mother, a drunken brother, and a gambling brother in Bangkok, who was supposed to take care of the family. We are all living for the sake of living. Everybody eats. Everybody drinks. Everybody sleeps. But what is the quality of life? Well, I don't know. I was in the village mode. Let me understand the urban jungle's law of survival of the fittest.

I was lost. I was satisfied in finding food, taking care of children, working in the land, and I was surviving. I was pleased only when somebody would arrive from the big cities. I used to listen to the stories they told of all the great things available in the urban areas.

I was slowly told by a friend of mine who was working in a massage shop in Pattaya City that I was wasting my life, my youth, my beauty in sitting in this place and working in the field. I had been living without a husband for many, many years now. He had already married another lady who had a daughter with someone else, and he was very happy having his sexual life with that lady. He would come once in a while to visit his children and would give a small amount of money to them or some small gifts and then get away. He would not even look at me though I was his darling wife for many years.

I was no good for him. He was finished with me. He had drunk all the nectar of my youth. Now, I was a middle-aged lady, but still I was very, very desirable as per my looks to many men in my village, who would look at me with greed and hunger. I was so angry with me, my family, and the whole world, but what good would my anger bring? Was there a salvation from all my miseries? I decided, *Enough of these sob stories of a hapless girl*. I should awake, arise, and not stop till

I achieved my goal of making big money. I had heard many stories of folks from ordinary and humble backgrounds who virtually achieved great feats in the flow of life. I trusted my husband implicitly that we would cross that bridge together. My faith in the institute of marriage was shaken. Men use women as long as they are attractive and dump them when they are not needed any more.

I started thinking, *What is the best way to earn money?* Having once been a maidservant in Bangkok, I think I have passed that stage to take care of children at the home of others. I needed to earn a good amount, and for that, I decided to take up a massage girl's job. My friend from Pattaya had told me it is a decent job, a noble job, wherein you are helping people to relax and get relief from pain. We would get a percentage from the charges and varied tips from satisfied customers. In a day, we might get four to five customers; it varied depending on the season and transit of tourists. All put together, it would give me a good amount to pursue my dream to become rich and famous. You have to dream big to get what you want from life and follow it up steadfastly and conscientiously to reach the target. My life had taught me a big lesson—that I should not trust anybody blindly and to think of the pros and cons to arrive at a decision.

My experience of men is basically the same all these years of my life. All men claim that they are civilized, polite, and understanding, but at any opportunity offered, they will take whatever is available to fulfil their sexual appetites. I managed to be a virgin when I got married to this great husband of mine, with whom I had a very good life and produced two children.

So going back to my predicament in my family life, where money was not available, I decided to take the advice of my friend who was working in Pattaya City. It's called the city of joy, city of sin. The city of possibilities was calling me to try my luck. This lady friend of mine was willing to take me and assured me that she would get me a massage job.

My parents had no problem in sending me because they were in need of money. Money was always needed. Money was the balm to heal all our aches and pains. I asked my children that I would go away to Pattaya and leave them all to earn money so that they could go to school, to a better school, and have lots of books, more of chicken, more of pork. They were not ready to start with, but all our village friends, neighbours, and relatives told that it would be good for the family if I go to make money.

I got into a bus from the village to Bangkok, a journey of ten to eleven hours, and went to Bangkok and then, from there, another two hours to Pattaya. My friend took me to a massage shop whose owner was a smart lady. Generally, most of the massage shops in Pattaya and in other cities of Thailand are owned by ladies. They are ex-massage girls who met a rich lovable foreigner who wanted to become their boyfriend and gave them money just like that. There are many ladies who have boyfriends from all over the world.

They give them money to develop that attachment and to build a long-term relationship. Five fingers can give different money. Some of them are kind, some are hard, some are cunning, some are generous, some are good, some are bad, but generally, everybody wants sex. Everybody wants the best, all the heat of one's accumulated passions to be released. If one cannot find a suitable female for him to copulate with in his country, he goes to Thailand. They use these young bodies to satiate their urge two times, three times, I don't know—any number of times.

The lady who has the strength, the courage, the feeling to withstand all these physical onslaughts in all sexual activities with a smile to get that money. I don't know who made money. I know the old system of barter was there when they used to exchange goods for goods, but now it is paper currency for all services.

I was introduced to this lady who owned a few massage shops in Pattaya. She was a good, intelligent lady with a good heart. She had a nice figure and great mannerisms. She heard my story, but she was not hearing anything new. It was the same old story for all the little women who come in at their middle age. With two children or one child or no child or at thirty to forty-five years old, they wanted to make money and send money to their parents who were in need of it for their day-to-day expenses. She trained me up to be a massage girl. I was put in one of the smaller branches of hers to work, learn, and apply the same on customers.

All Thai girls learn massage early because they are used to massaging the feet or the body of their elders. Whether it is the grandmother, uncle, aunt, mother, father, or anybody that has any pain in their bodies, the girls would take care of them by massaging them. It's a physical activity that soothes the frayed nerves of the body. Every lady basically knows what a massage is and how to do massage, so I picked up the trade. The hands on the finer points of the tired body give the much-needed relaxation. Once I had learned the finer points of massage, they took care of my grooming; it was more important for me to look sexy.

Actual massage depends on the needs of the customer—their age, their size, their skin, and their flexibility—and whether the customer's requirement is a light touch or a hard touch or a very strong touch. Basically, the presentation is a great gift from the Western culture to the ancient culture of the East. The amount of make-up you are supposed to do to look pretty is awesome.

In the village, we would wash our faces and take our showers with soap in the morning, in the afternoon, or maybe in the night. Two, three times we would take a shower, and that was it. But once you are in the city and especially if you're a massage girl, you have to become attractive to the men and women who come to get a massage done. The low-light atmosphere, air conditioner working, and a nicely uniformed girl in a T-shirt with the upper button open and her cleavage showing will excite them. You are made up. Your eyebrows, your eye lashes, your cheeks are rouged, powdered, painted, lipstick on your lips, and your hair is nicely groomed. All in all, you're supposed to look and behave as a sexy lady.

In any field of work, marketing a product is very important, and that only brings in the customers.

We were young, attractive, desirable. All the girls in the massage shop were ready by ten in the morning, and we were waiting for the customers. In a small shop, you'll have four, five girls, and in a big shop, it can be twenty girls, thirty girls. The girls who do not have a customer sit on the roadside of the shop, presenting themselves to the passing customers and to the tourists who are visiting the great Pattaya City.

The men who come in to get a massage can choose which girl will do the massage for him. For a foot massage, you are in the open on the ground floor, where many nice recliners are put; they are adjustable for the foot to be massaged. The price varies from location to location, place to place, and star hotel to star hotel. The foot massage is basically a clean massage on the tired legs of a tourist, who goes around sightseeing, and it is a welcome relief from pain.

The lady prepares the customer for the foot massage by washing both legs with soap water, making them supple for the procedure. She applies some softening solution and some Tiger balm and slowly starts rubbing the foot. The man looks at the girl, and the girl smiles. The girl asks 'Light? Strong? Are you okay?' in broken English. I started learning it as I did not pay attention to my English classes in my school—*strong, hard*, whatever my English could convey to the customer. I picked up from the seniors whatever they would say to the customers, and I would also repeat it like a parrot.

There's a Thai massage where the whole body is given a dry massage, and there is an oil massage where your whole body is massaged with oils, special oil, aroma oil, spa therapy, and so on. For all other massages, you are taken to the first floor or the second floor. After changing clothes, the whole activity starts. Massages are done with the nimble hands of a well-trained lady who in the process is taught the trick to excite the man or the woman. It's 90 per cent hard work, and 10 per cent is when you bring in a touch of sex.

The men are excited, and most of them are in Thailand for the erotica and for a good sexual experience. Both are available; it is your choice. There was no masturbation done in our massage shop. Even if a customer wanted it, any sexual activity was a no-no for most of them at our shops. There are exceptions wherein you pay three times, five times more than the normal money you pay for a massage. For a masturbation, the slang word is *chakla*. There are some shops who offer a variety of shows and services where you can get all the gigs. There are many live shows, pole dances, and variety of other dances.

There are many other shops and big establishments with the blessing of the influential who have some thirty, forty girls who squat in a glass studio. It is a mini stadium with steps wherein they wear a badge with a number and sit. Customers come, and they choose whom they want. They are taken away, and they are taken care of with a body massage, breast massage, sex, anything they want for a price.

Well, by luck, I did not go into that. I didn't want to. I felt that I needed to earn the money to take care of my family by serving the men and the women who come for a massage. I would make them happy, and I would make my money from their generous tips. Sometimes there was no tip, and sometimes there's little tip, but of course, everybody gave some amount of money apart from the percentage I would get from my boss for the services that I performed.

I was getting three, four, five customers a day as per my turn. There were many other girls who also had to get customers on the rotation basis. Live and let live was the policy. The boss took a percentage to run the shop— clean sheets, clean towels, electricity, water, perfumes, soap bubbles, oil, powder, rent, salaries to cashier, housekeeping staff—and then for her profits.

There are thousands of massage shops all over Thailand catering to the needs of millions of happiness seekers. Thailand is the land of a thousand smiles. We are there to serve the rich and moneyed guys. Yes, we need that money; that's what keeps us going.

I started my life like that, and I graduated from the small shop to the big shop of my boss, where they were ten to fifteen girls working. They all would start working at ten a.m. in the morning and end up working up to one a.m. in the night—no working hours. We we're supposed to work. We we're supposed to make money. We had no other business there. We had no personal life. We had no personal needs. Our needs were put into the back-burner.

We we're there for twenty-four hours, and we thought in terms of money. Money was what prompted us to work. To work—that was the only motto. That was my obsession to keep on working. My boss was impressed with me in a few months; she was pleased with my work, the way I picked up my trade. I was searched out by many repeat customers and the locals. Life became interesting. I was given a better place to stay in with only a few girls in the room instead of many.

My boss started treating me with a little respect. She was a very friendly lady. She started telling me, 'You're here to make money. Don't lose your focus, and do not get into other activities in your spare time.'

There was no spare time. We would sleep at around two a.m. in the night, get up at eight o'clock, and get ready for work. We were hungry in the morning, we used to eat rice with pork quickly and got ready to be on duty at ten o'clock. There were no choices. The wheel of time kept on rolling for better times. I was having better food. I was having a better time with my same-age group.

There are many, many stories of how many girls marry many Europeans who have chosen them as their permanent girlfriends. Most of the Europeans and Americans who come to live in Pattaya for two months, three months, six months will find and choose a suitable girl, and she will live with him after her working hours. Sometimes, she gives up her job and goes to live with him if he compensates her with the amount of money which is much more than what she can make in the massage shop. It's all a permutation and combination of how much money she can produce in one month for her family's needs.

The money went regularly to my parents. Their standard of life improved, and the demand for money increased. The children wanted many other facilities. My second son wanted a cycle to go to school; he had been walking all these years. My first son wanted a motorbike right away because we had many small ones, which were reasonably priced. More the money I had, more the demand from my children, from my parents, and from my relatives.

Now basically, I was making more money now than in the beginning of six months. I knew how to take care of a customer, how to speak to them, how to understand their issues, how to make them happy. I was transferred to another shop. My boss had a branch which was attached to a hotel, and that was how I got promoted. I for one was totally focused on my work. I had become a machine for producing money. My customers were happy, the other girls in the shop were happy, my boss was happy, so what else was required? My family was also happy with the money I was sending them every month.

Chapter 6

I started dressing better as time moved on. I was doing good in the hotel branch and had a good reputation. There was an option for the hotel guests to call the massage girls to their rooms for a massage. They needed their privacy, and at the same time, they wanted to feel that exclusiveness in their own room's comfort. This was what I was told by the seniors and my boss. Of course, the boss was charging extra money for this. At the same time, the hotel was charging extra money for allowing the masseuse to go in and work in the hotel room.

There were many old women, many old men who wanted to have an exclusive massage. I was wearing a white coat as my uniform, and I carried a kit which contained the oil for the massage, powder, massage tools like the wooden sticks used to prod the soul of the feet, the napkins, and so on. These were the tools of my trade, and I would go to the sixth floor, third floor, or eighth floor and knock on the rooms. The door would open, and the person would call me in whether it was a male or a female.

The customer would undress and lie down. I would do the massage. It was normally for one hour, and the fees were charged. In a star hotel in a bigger city, it would be for half an hour; you could have multiples of half hour or multiples of one hour. The more money you gave, the more time you could get a massage. Normally, many would get two hours of oil massage as long as they were comfortable and feeling relaxed.

After the massage, they were really gracious. The money was paid with a good tip or a mediocre tip, and I would say thank you or *Kha pun kha* in Thai.

I was feeling great. I could make that extra one hundred baht. That is the currency of Thailand, like a dollar. I was waiting for the extra visits to the rooms because I could get more money than working in the shop. I was visiting many male and female customers in the rooms and carrying out my job very diligently. Time went by, and one day there was a call by a customer to visit him in his room for a massage. The cashier told me it was my turn to go to the room and asked me to go immediately. I wore my white coat, took my tools of the trade, and reached the room of the customer. I knocked on the room, and the door was opened immediately. I was grabbed, and he started molesting me. I tried to make him understand that I was a massage girl and that there were other girls available for this purpose at many shops. I just did not succeed in putting some sense in him. He was so powerful physically. He was so animalistic, and he ravished me. I couldn't do a damn thing about it. He was crazy and keyed up to have me; he just needed a female body. I think there are many men who think females have no role or say in the act of sex. I couldn't protect myself. My body went through the motions.

What the hell could I do? This is the story of many, many, many young girls not only in Thailand but all over the world. The haves with the greater money, the greater wealth do this to all the poor, all the have-nots, servants, office staff; even their wives go through it. We call it rape, but not everybody uses the word *rape* these days, and nobody is bothered. Even in the rich countries, all the money-needing ones are raped. Who the hell can stop this?

So long as ordinary men are there, so long as rich men are there, so long as starved men are there, the women are exploited. I was crying uncontrollably. That man threw money at me, and he did not care about me. I picked up the money he threw at me. He didn't even have the grace to put it in my hand. I felt ashamed. My flesh was crawling, like thousands of scorpions were biting me, but I couldn't help it. I went out of the room, and I was wondered and meditated on what happened to me.

I did enjoy what happened to me, when that man forcibly took me. I felt ashamed of myself. I was wondering how he managed to wear a condom, which protected me. At the same time, I felt that my stupid body is made out of so many chemicals, hormones, and what other names the scientists have given them today that my body reacted forcibly, and I realized I had an orgasm a long, long time after my husband left me. I was totally dormant in my sexual activity after my second child's birth. I had sealed my sexual life, and it was in a coma. Now I was jolted and awakened.

I used to get aroused. I use to feel sexual, but I never had an intercourse in all these years. Then suddenly, I was taken forcibly, and I enjoyed the force. I enjoyed the penetration in my vagina, the tool of that guy into my vagina, and I had multiple orgasms. I was totally wet. Pain, pleasure, pain—what a combination! I was bruised. All my friends asked me, 'Why? What happened?' I said nothing to anybody. What was the point? I took some water; luckily, I had no customer to massage.

I took some rest, and on that day, I had some beer with my friends. They were all having beer every day, and many had different, different stories of their own. They had gone into a friendship, a partnership with liquor. After a hard day's work from 10 a.m. to 1 a.m. and around that time, midnight, they would drink a little beer and go to sleep because they were tired; that was what they claimed.

Most of the poor people in any trade today—whether it is in construction, work in agricultural activity, or carrying loads of weight like a donkey—all become very good friends with liquor. All these liquor is manufactured by the very rich. All the hard-earned money goes into the pockets of the very rich to make them stinking rich. The big business houses control the intelligent fellows, who run very big business houses and who in turn control the majority of the poor. I'm not against rich people.

That is what economics is. The logic works, and who the hell has made all this? He's called the god. This power, it has put everybody in a different slot—some high, some low, some middle. What is the drama? Everybody says we are all actors in the theatre of life. We come to act, we finish acting, and then we go back. Where the hell do we go back to— heaven or hell? No one knows. No one has seen it, including the godly men of all the guys. Nobody has seen it; it's an imagination. It is a thought of some intelligent guy who has told all this to make the people accept the power, the god as our saviour and as our stress buster; he is all in all the father figure to all of us. Where is the mother?

I was frustrated, and at the same time, I was pleased to have had my multiple orgasms. I felt rejuvenated. I felt nice, pepped up, and all my frustrations were removed. I was high in my meditation. I felt I was seeing my god, my Buddha, and my whole body was light. I was in seventh heaven, sixth heaven, or whatever heaven you have. I felt very, very happy, and it was the feeling that I had with my husband on my first night. It was beautiful having sex with him, enjoyable, and

I was so happy and pleased. Now, I understood why food tastes great when your are starving. I think my dormant sexuality was too eager to lap it up.

I was wondering why it happened to me. I came in to earn money for my family. By doing the job, I could take care of my kids, parents, and relatives in my own small way. What right did that man have to do what he did to me just because he had money and brute force and was he a man or what? I don't know. Even in this, I learned a hard lesson that whatever has to happen will happen. We cannot change it. It was my fate that I was to be taken forcibly by that guy.

I started feeling after a period of nine years or maybe nine and a half years. I tasted sex forced upon me. I'm ashamed to say I did enjoy it, though I resisted it in the beginning. I enjoyed it not because the guy was great or anything like that. It was because my body reacted to the stimuli, and my response was my orgasm. The great doctor Pavlov's theory of stimuli and response would not be a friend of mine.

I now trust older guys because they're not brutal; they're more experienced. They know how to get the job done maybe in their own cunning way, but they're nice to people. They cannot perform as well as the brute young man, but they're nice. They give you more pleasure than a youngster who is physically strong. So that's how it is. You cannot expect a hot-headed young man to behave in a decent way. It may only be in my isolated case or maybe in minority of cases that it happens like that. In general, the older men are safer, easier to handle, and they need the support of us to take care of them to fulfil their needs for their own sexual drive. The drive may be very high, but their bodies may not be capable of producing that kind of result as per their desire.

After the trauma of the sudden assault on my body, I became smarter. I slowly spoke to many of my friends and to my boss of what happened. They told me that in the business, when you are going alone to do a massage for a person, whether they're young or old, you're exposed to these kinds of situations, so you should be prepared mentally to face it. In the four walls of the shop, nothing will happen because there are many other customers and many other girls who are doing the job. You shouldn't take this assignment if you're not capable of protecting yourself, or you should give in to the desires of the customer, which in turn can fetch you more money.

I analysed and understood that what they said was true. I thought whether I should restrict myself to the shop or I could take up the job to go to the room of the customer. It took me some time to understand and appreciate the way the massage industry works or a business operates, wherein you're exposed to humans with different emotions and needs. Different people react differently to a given situation. In the process, I decided that I could earn maybe five times more than what I was earning right now just as a massage lady. I decided that I would start going into rooms with proper protection and with plenty of guts. Many were just for massage, many were for happy endings, and many were too eager to have sex. Many fellows were aggressive, but I tamed them by being aggressive by showing them my pepper spray and telling them that I could complain to the police.

Things fell into place. I could handle any situation, and my English had improved. I could speak better and make customers understand my need. Their need was there, but my need was more important to me, and it was a business transaction. I should get what I want or at least my negotiated price. Many wanted sex with me, and I gave in to them all if they paid the correct price to get all the goodies of this great body of mine and my activity. That's how it is—people have needs, and I have my needs.

I started making more money than I was before. My boss was pleased. I was in demand. I started getting more money. In a year's time, I went back to my place to visit my people. They were all very, very pleased that I was looking good—maybe slightly worn out but good. For their pleasures, people who had the best of scotch, the best of food shared the same with me, hoping that I would be very nice to them. It's always in the psyche of a man to make a lady happy, and in the process, they will make them happy; it is very true. It's Newton's third law of motion: 'Every action will have an equal and opposite reaction.'

Chapter 7

My people were very happy. I had the prettiest clothes, goodies, and small, small gifts to all friends, relatives, neighbours, friends of friends, parents, children; all were very happy with me. I was happy to see there was a bit of gratitude, happiness in their faces.

My drunkard brother got extra money from me for him to drink more because he wouldn't change. We all tried our best, but he was not willing to change. He would say, 'I won't drink,' but he would drink. Well, again it is the fate of that gentleman, I don't know. He's my sibling; he's my blood. But he's like that, and I'm like this. I was not happy to be at home. No money came in; there was only money spent. I had to pay for all the extra needs, and I wanted to get back to Pattaya City, which de-stresses all the people who goes to it. It is the city that makes visitors very happy, and all go back very happily to their own hellholes or heaven. We have seen hellholes, but no one has seen heaven.

Okay, at the beginning of my second year, I had a customer who came with his friend. He and his friend asked for a massage in our shop. This man was middle-aged. He had some kind of charisma and charm around him. As my customer, he looked at me as though I was a princess or an apsara (divine damsel) from heaven. He was very, very polite and very, very nice and very good in all his mannerisms.

At the same time, he was generous with his purse, and he gave me good tips. It was high by the standards of a normal customer. He was looking at me all the time. He was very excited. He kept on talking to me. I couldn't understand him, only very few words. He came again three times in a day for a massage, then he took the lead and called me for a massage in his room.

He asked my cashier, the person in charge of the shop, 'Can I have this lady massage me in my room?'

She said, 'Yes.'

And I was asked to go to his room in the hotel. I was happy to go because I was comfortable with that gentleman. I wore my coat, took my tools of the trade, went to his room, and knocked on his door. He opened the door with a big smile and welcomed me with a handshake. I was offered a seat, and he asked me hesitantly whether he could have sex with me. I told him my price. He offered me a drink, and I took it to please him. He very hurriedly counted his money, but he was short of some money. He said he was short of money and that he would change his money from dollars to baht and give it to me the next day as it was too late in the night, then we could have sex the next day. He looked very sad, and his disappointment was clear on his face.

I saw something in him. I told him that whatever he had he could give it to me now and that it was okay. He could give the balance the next day.

He said, 'No, no. Tomorrow first thing in the morning, I'll give you the balance.'

He offered me a clean towel, and I was asked to be comfortable. I felt he was so nice to me. I had the feeling of meeting somebody who was known to me, somebody who was very close to me, somebody who was more considerate towards me than my own ex-husband.

I went into the bathroom, changed, and came out with a towel wrapped around me. He was patiently waiting for me and held my hand and led me to the bed. He asked my permission to unrobed me and slowly started kissing me all over my body. He was weaving a magic on me; his slow and firm movements were playing havoc on my emotions. I was high with sexual desire, which was getting enhanced, and he was making many sounds of happiness. I was getting due attention on all my assets. My breasts were swelling, and my nipples were taut, wanting more attention. He was an experienced master of the art of coitus; his movements and touch were arousing me. I was holding his erect penis, which was strong and stiff. I made him lie down, took it in my mouth, and started sucking it. He was in great pleasure, goading me through his eyes to make him happy. I took the cue in giving him what he wanted. At some stage, he asked me to stop as he was very high. He tore open a condom to put it on. I helped him out with it, and he took me straight with a smooth penetration.

There was no brute force or great hurry in entering me; at the same time, there was a great need to perform and reach the pinnacle. He was moving inside me with varied movements of his body. There was strength, but it was flexible; he kept on building me up. I was asked whether I was ready for the finals. I said yes. He was full of love, and all his experience, patience in making a partner happy was all evident. We moved furiously to achieve the crescendo to be one with the maker—that is, the meditation. We exploded like a bomb when we achieved our orgasms. I was pouring out my cum, and I was wet all over. He must have kissed me a hundred times. He thanked me profusely for the wonderful time. I reciprocated the same feelings towards him.

We were all smiles, and that was the beginning of a great friendship. I felt he was my soulmate (I don't have many of these expressions), like I'd been talking to this friend of mine for the last nine years who came to me regularly. He patiently taught me correct English, and now I could understand many words. I could interact on most subjects. I felt really comfortable with him, and I felt I was with someone I'd known for a long time.

The Asians of the Hindu and Buddhist faiths believe in many births to attain salvation. In the process, they meet many souls with whom they continue their relationships through many births. Maybe he was my mate from a previous birth or he was my soulmate. Sometimes you feel immensely happy when you meet a stranger or hate a person at the very first sight, and that is due to the connections from previous births.

Chapter 8

The second encounter with my soulmate, my boyfriend, was out of this world after the episode of abstaining from sex for a period of nine years. The encounter with this friend of mine whom I call as my soul mate was very gracious. He asked me to change, and I went into the bathroom and came out in my birthday suit. He was all ready, with his eyes full of love and affection. I saw no brute force. I saw no hurry in touching me or taking me.

There's a lot of difference between a young man and a middle-aged man or an old man. Maybe it's because they're experienced. Maybe it is because they have many denial modes from their whimsical wives. They are used to sleeping alone and turning to the other side though their wives are present on the bed. Many of these guys have told me many stories that after they have a child, their wives do not cooperate; many say they are very busy with the child, especially those in Asia. The lady sleeps with the child in the bed, and the husband is on the other side. Yes, there's a lot of affection towards the child, and it is nice, but the man also needs care. The lady has her own problems—taking care of the house, taking care of the children—refuses to have sex.

The frustrated friend of mine made me sit. My English was not up to the mark, and he was speaking rapidly, animatedly. He slowly started touching me, fondling me, kissing me in a very delicate manner. I was feeling goose bumps on my body. He was so slow and nice; his touch was nice.

He made me lie down, and he started slowly sucking my nipples. I felt my breasts starting to swell in anticipation. I started feeling whether it was my ex-husband who had come back, but well, he had gone to another woman. This man started feeling me, touching me. Slowly he was building me up. I wondered, *Am I getting excited? Am I starting to enjoy sex?* Yes was the answer.

He started kissing me from my head to toe, from the front, from the rear. He was licking me all over. It was a very different taste, a very different feeling. I was getting excited. He wore a condom and slowly entered me. It was smooth; he was an experienced person. He applied a lot of his saliva on to his penis, and there was no pain. He adopted a different posture instead of the normal missionary one. I started feeling excited; he started moving slowly and steadily. The feeling was great; my body was trembling. Already I had an orgasm, and the cum was trickling down. Maybe I was made to enjoy sex. My body was taking in all the inputs of the thrust. I started moaning.

Suddenly, he stopped.

I said, 'What?'

He said, 'Wait.'

He changed to another position, and he entered me again. That was a new position for me. I was used to only one position all the time with my husband. Here, my friend said that there are sixty-nine postures as per the Kama Sutra, an Indian book on sexual acts. I felt I was building up to another orgasm. Maybe I was too quick to orgasm or maybe I was enjoying it, I don't know. That was my experience.

Finally, he took another position. He was strong, and his penis was much, much longer—maybe seven, eight inches. Maybe it was possible to have variations with a bigger penis. He was a tall man, and many additional positions were possible for a tall man. Finally, we both came together. It was a big, big explosion. He was shouting. I was shouting. There was no one to tell us to stop because it was a big air-conditioned room. There was no one to question us. We could shout on the top of our voices. That was my soul-stirring encounter with him; that was great.

He was very nice to me and said, 'Stay until I withdraw from you.'

It took five minutes. He slowly withdrew, offered me tissues, and told me to go and clean myself. Then as soon as I came out of the bathroom, he went in and washed himself. We dressed, and we both hugged each other. He kissed me, I kissed him, and there was a bond building up. There was a friendship, and I felt this friendship was going to last for a long time to come.

I was very eager to be with him because I felt there was a lot of variety, a lot of adventure, a lot of different postures that were possible with him, which gave me lots of happiness. I'm not denying it, not trying to be modest and saying that I do not enjoy sex. I do enjoy sex. I enjoy sex because it gives me a lot of relaxation; it gives me a lot of happiness. More than that, it gives me my bread butter and maybe jam in time to come.

Later, whenever he visited me, it was a memorable event. I was waiting for him to come, and the minute I set my eyes on him, my heart skipped a beat. I was so excited and full of anticipation. We enjoyed sex together for two hours at a time without stopping. We tried maybe twenty different postures, and we tried to do a lot of difficult things together. We enjoyed each other's company very much. It was not sex all the time; it was more of the feeling of comfort our proximity was producing. We felt the calmness and happiness that our togetherness was bringing into our lives. Life can be one pure bliss with someone you like, and you feel that time should stop for all eternity to come. My life had taken such a drastic turn for the good from the recent miseries.

After two, three years of our friendship, I offered for him not to wear a condom so he could enter me straight because I was clean and I was protecting myself. I had no diseases, and I was sure my boyfriend was also safe, him being a family man. He assured me that he did not go to anybody, let alone a girl who was easily available.

I asked him, 'How come you came to me?'

He said, 'You are a massage girl, and I could see the spark in your eyes that you are a very new entrant to this profession of massage.'

He said that he knew how I protected myself from my customers. He had made his survey, I suppose. There are many girls who are there only for sex. But most of the massage girls are also willing to have sex in a customer's room depending on the money, I suppose. We were great together. He told me that he was also clean. There was no problem, and we both trusted each other. We were having sex without any protection. Of course, I was taking care of my periods and avoiding any chance of pregnancy.

We also had sex in the bathtub when I had a period. It was a little messy, but for greater urge and variety, you can always try it out. We did many different postures; all were very enjoyable. It was interesting to see the turn my life had taken, from where to where—from a married life in the village, then a massage shop, then meeting a guy who was bad to me, and now a person nice to me. How and why all these had happened, there was no answer to these. My friend gave me answers to many things. He said, 'All good will come. Just believe in the universe. You do good karma, you get good results. You do bad karma, you get bad results.'

All this is told by the religious people, the monks, the priests. Again, it's a question mark what is good, what is bad, why some have all the goodies, and why some don't have anything. Again, it is a matter of each one's situation; that was what my friend told me. When your mind says when you do a wrong as a wrong, that is your cue to know the good and bad.

Suffice it to say, we enjoyed all our sexual outings. We continued to travel within Thailand. We had reached a stage where we perfectly understood each other, and we were having a synchronized sexual life. Both were made for each other, and there were always good marks—eight out of ten. We would reach the pinnacle that high in sexual life. Today, I know many couples are having a bad time. With our minds, our bodies, it is a matter of give and take and understanding the person's needs. Most of the men, whether they are drunk or not, are too eager. Their mind-set is to touch, fondle, enter, pour, finish, and get out. It is a similar situation with the wives; married men do not give time, nor do they understand the needs of their partners. Unfortunately, there are so many frigid women, women who do not know that they can get an orgasm.

I have met many guys and many females who might want a massage, and when I massage a lady, there are many who have told me, 'I'm feeling nice. I'm feeling good. My husband never takes care of me.' Other guys complain that they're all a frustrated lot. They do not know nor do they strive for the pleasure angle or do not know how to enjoy a proper sex life. If a woman asks for sex, people will say she's a loose woman, that she's not a good woman. Can she not tell her preferences, feelings? Can she not share her happiness? It's such a lopsided approach to sexual practices.

Today the greatest villains for the happiness in our sexual lives are the taboos of the moralistic brigade of good, bad, and ugly. Why is sex being depicted as a very ugly and very harsh subject? It is one's private matter to have in their privacy, and no one has the right to question it. Why is it not being discussed, explained to the men and women of this world? I have seen, met, heard a lot of people who go as tourists to Thailand, all feeling that they've never had a proper sex life. There are many live sexy shows—like *Alcazar, Tiffany*— and other activities performed on the stage in Pattaya City, Thailand. They also have many live adult shows on the stage, where a man and a woman have sex.

There are many adult shows where a woman opens a bottle of cola using her vagina, smokes a cigarette from her vagina, or blows a small arrow from her vagina so that it goes and pierces a balloon. All that show great muscle control and practice, which makes a person perfect. People go to these shows eagerly, wanting, demanding, swallowing their false prides and the fear of stigma of the society and family. Long live the rules, regulations, and hypocrisy of this society.

Chapter 9

He knew what was going on. He knew that I was massaging other men. I was with other men for other activities, but still he wanted me despite knowing this and paid me my price.

One time he asked me, 'Are you healthy? Do you have any health issues?'

I said, 'Yes, I am healthy, and I practise safe sex.'

I'd always insisted on using condoms with my customers. Not all encounters ended up with sex; only a minority ended with sex, majority with only massage, and the middle order only with happy endings. There was no other problem. He understood and appreciated it and said he was very happy. He wished that he had enough money so he could stop me from working as a massage lady. If wishes are horses; everybody will ride it. I thanked him for his love, kindness, affection, and good feelings for my welfare. My destiny is to be a massage lady, and I remain so by the will of Buddha. I may be wrong. Lord Buddha may have surprises waiting for me. He holds the key for my future.

The third year of my massage work gave me more experience in this line of work, meeting men and women day in and day out. I became a very good psychiatrist or psychoanalyst. I didn't need to master many languages to understand all men of all nationalities. Whosoever came to me, I would massage them. I called on them in their rooms for a happy ending and no sexual intercourse because they wanted to protect themselves. Fine. Many guys will not have sex with an easy prey or easy person or those they call with the name prostitute or easy virtue or unvirtuous woman—whatever titles are there. Just because you're available at their beck and call, you're a fallen woman, not a good woman. You're a bad woman, a prostitute, and they will never have sex with you.

They want the body. They want to feel it. They want to suck it. They want to do anything but not the intercourse because they're scared the condom will burst; they want to protect their wives, of course. Fine. Good. Let them say hallelujah. It's the single-partner theory, the double standards of no sexual intercourse, but they will have a happy ending. Some will want the blow job; this is available. But anything hard to get or anything wherein you have to struggle to get is what is prized, and you will spend anything to get it. Anything easy, no one wants. Anything and everything tough or difficult is what men want; that includes women also.

So I kept on understanding these things. One time, my friend was there. He had finished an activity or one session with me and was in my shop, talking to the other girls because he was popular with the others and he was my boyfriend. He sat and chatted with them. One Middle Eastern man had come for a massage, and I was working on him. The boyfriend of mine was so worked up. He was looking at me when I closed the screen to work on that guy. He was fidgeting. My lady friend said, 'Open the screen.' I opened it. I finished my massage, and that customer while going asked me to go to his room; I felt hesitant for one minute. I felt that I was cheating on my boyfriend, but my boyfriend was not

LIFE OF A THAI MASSEUSE   67

my husband. My boyfriend would be there maybe for a week and then go away back to his environment.

What would I do? What would my family eat? My commitment was to them. Already, for many years, I had taken care of them, and they were very, very happy that I was taking care of them. Money was available, but I brushed aside my feelings. I had no opportunity to have any such luxuries.

My cashier, the manager, said, 'Go to his room.' So and so, I had to go without questioning.

I told him, 'Take care. See you tonight.'

I went, took my coat, put it on, took all my tools of the trade, and went to that room number. He was so angry. He said bye to my older friends.

They said, 'Take it easy. She'll be back in one hour's time.'

He went away. It so happened that I was shacked up with that man, who took me for four hours. I was bound to be with him. I couldn't say no because he paid for four hours. What choice did I have? Could I have said no? I would have been removed from my job. Where would I go? I would have to start again from zero.

Next day, as soon as I went to the shop, my boyfriend was waiting. He booked me and took me for two hours to his room. He was crying. I cried. We both cried. We both felt we needed each other; we liked each other. We might be soulmates but not money mates. Both of us did not have sufficient funds. He could not afford to leave his background. He could not support me as long as he was alive, or I could leave all this and be with him all the time. But I had my commitment to my family, and I had to take care of them. I didn't have that kind of money. We understood the reality. We were happy to be together for now. We did not even think of having sex; it was a little beyond that. We were starting, yeah, a relationship between husband and wife or between two lovers or between two soulmates. I didn't know what the hell it was, but anyway, we were together all the time. I spent three hours with him though he was charged only for two hours. I told my manager I was with him; they understood, and they let it go.

Small, small money is needed; you need a fraction of a US dollar to get rice, a fraction of a dollar to get soup. That's what the majority Thais eat with greens, with mushrooms. It's a luxury sometimes to have chicken, pork, fish. Money is scarce. Most of the girls in this trade spend only half a dollar for their lunch and half a dollar for their dinner. Sometimes they get it from their customers—free dinner and a bit of liquor. This is what is happening, and the money saved goes into clothing, grooming, taking care of one's body. A bit of money goes to the doctor for all the problems you may get with a human body. You can get fever, headache, body aches. You need lotions to keep your skin soft and smooth; you need make-up to look beautiful. The first look is what is important. You should be beautiful and presentable, and only then will you be picked up for the work.

Chapter 10

I felt that there was a glimmer of hope in my life when I met someone who gave me a bit of happiness. He made me understand many of his point of views in improving myself; he made me go to learn English in school. He paid the money for it, for me to speak, read, and write. I gave up after three months because I couldn't write, but I had learned a little to read. Speaking was good—okay, good enough to survive in my trade. Then slowly I had a feeling that I had met someone who was going to be with me for a long time. I remembered his words of how there's a feeling or awareness that there is an inner being who resides in us whom we call as the god and who will guide us to our destiny. I used to laugh at him and say I didn't understand his philosophy.

He would tell me, 'We have a body, we have a mind, we have an intellect. It is called BMI, and then we have the fourth state. That is the being or atman or the god, and it's dormant but witnesses with no role to play in our lives.'

There's a practice all over Asia wherein persons who meet other persons will fold both their hands and bend their heads and say hi. That is the traditional salute to the god who resides in you. The body, the mind, and the intellect do all the other works. All the decisions are taken by them; all the pleasures and pain are enjoyed by them. I felt that my guy, my soulmate, gave me confidence that I can improve. I can have new horizons in my life, and I can change myself to be a better human being.

I felt that I might not have the capacity or calibre to understand the intricacies of life. Why not? Even the smallest person can be better; for that, you have to listen to your inner voice. There is something in you which says 'This is okay' or 'This is not okay'. You should listen to it. You should understand. Hostility, what is that hostility? A person always opposes any good advice because no one wants any unsolicited advice. You must try to understand the circumstances and the reason for the same. You should control your emotions. You should be able to deny certain things to yourself. The craving, anything you like very much, you should say no to it. That denial mode should be developed in you. Only when you deny yourself will you become strong.

Today, it is felt that the Westerners are more fortunate, the Westerners have a better standard of life with better wages. Mother Nature has blessed them with a lot of natural resources. All their basic needs are taken care of, and they have enough time to do creative work for the good or bad of humans. They have brains, they have intelligence, they have patience, and they have money. Their one dollar can buy thirty-two baht; one is equal to thirty-two. That is a lot of purchasing power.

When you speak, your voice goes up or down. Your voice varies depending on your stress and feelings, so you have to practise denial mode; that will make you a better person. You cannot get everything you want; nobody can give them to you however rich you are. Whatever you are destined to have, you will receive only that however affluent you are. So once you develop that denial mode, you're a better person. For Asians (especially Thais, Indians, Cambodians), all these people are so used to denial that if anything happens, they are not bothered; they just take it easy, and they just smile and get away. I started telling my people that I met a man, a middle-aged man with whom I was very, very happy and he's very nice to me and I feel comfortable with him. They were happy, and at the same time, they were unhappy. They were scared that I would go away with him. Definitely not—I would never.

My loyalty, my emotions, my feelings are with my family. My sons are very dear to me. My papa and mama are very dear to me. My personal happiness is secondary. I don't care if I lose him also. I'm practical. I told this to him, and he understood. He himself said whether he would come back next time or not, he did not know; he might be dead and gone. He advised me to marry somebody and settle down. It's a long story, and I'll make it short.

I told him, in Thailand, men marry young, when their sexuality is very high. After that, they produce one or two children, then they go to new pastures, where they find a new woman who is always willing. I've always felt that a woman is the villain of a woman. What are we to do? Everybody wants a man for their pleasures and for their survival. The best are always taken, and I told my people I had a great boyfriend.

The next time my friend came, my family had come to Pattaya to see me or to see the city or to eat better food. They were bored of eating the same food in the village. They came for two reasons. They could afford it now, and I could pay for their travel, their stay, their food, and all other minor wishes. They were curious to see my guy. They met my boyfriend; they liked him, and they were very pleased. At the same time, they asked me whether he was rich. I said, 'No, he's okay.

He can pay more price than what I normally earn.' They understood.

Then the best thing that happened to me was my boyfriend; everybody in the village knew I had a boyfriend, and they were all eager to see him. I asked him to come with me to my house to visit my family and friends. He agreed, and I took him to my village. My friend and relative went with my second son and my brother's daughter in his van to receive us. We drove down nearly sixty kilometres to my village. The whole village was there to welcome us. Sign language is the perfect bridge for the English and Thai conversations.

He had brought a lot of gifts and gave those to them. They happily accepted it. In Thailand, a lady alone—I suppose, anywhere in the world—is especially not very well respected. If she has a mate, a boyfriend (call him husband, call him anything), it's appreciated. Men have created this society where men have through the ages kept all the advantages in their favour because of their physical strength and their brute force. Men have two distinct advantages: they need not produce a baby, and their organ is external. But why does a female have two breasts and one vagina and a child-bearing sack and run the risk of going through unwanted pregnancies? Why should she have her period of twenty-eight days? Why should she have a uterus? Why should she produce an egg and have it meet a sperm for a child to take shape? The lady who produces a child is called a mother, who is responsible for continuing the human race and face all the challenges of motherhood. Why did the god do this? Why not for the man? Why the woman? Just because of her negativity or weaknesses in her body structure, through no fault of hers, she has to suffer so much.

My family and I were happy that I had found someone who understood me and supported me financially, morally, and physically. The main object was, of course, the money angle, the extra money which came in. It became my second income. My mother was dominating, and my father was docile, the general pattern in most families in Thailand. I was told or coached by my mother to earn more money and, at the same time, get more money from my boyfriend. I was hesitant; he was voluntarily giving me what he could. He said he was not a rich man, but he could support me to the best possible extent he could afford. He was paying me more than what I expected in the beginning of our relationship. As time passed, I had extra income from going out with my boss to entertain customers in the middle of the night. Mostly, it was with tiered businessmen who wanted a good body massage and a happy ending. We were less strained, and the money was good.

Whenever my boyfriend came, I would to take a holiday as and when it was required. It was the only time I was totally relaxed. I enjoyed my outings with him; my sexual fantasies were realized. My personal feelings, my needs were genuinely attended to by his sincere approach and warmth. I would feel very happy, and life was one great merry-go-around. My sexual appetite was totally satiated by him. I was forced to pay a sum of money to my boss when she said, 'You're making money from your boyfriend and missing the job. Revenue is affected.' Anyway, I agreed, and this practice went on for some time.

What interest I had developed in the sexual activity after nine and a half years of abstaining from sex after my husband left me became a mechanical affair with my customers. I was getting many bodies for massage, giving services to many customers, and entertaining guests with my boss in the night—three types of income. And when my boyfriend came, I had my fourth additional income.

Things were going on for the good. I was learning the trick of the trade—what to do, how to do it, when to do it, and when to stop. Life and its experiences are the biggest teachers for you to become smart, self-reliant, and at the same time, take care of your interests. Men go to you with a lot of interests. They are very nice to you. They want to touch you. They want to fondle you. They want to lick you. They want to hug you. They want to do so many things. When the passion or the urge subsides; it can be two minutes, five minutes, ten minutes, fifteen minutes, or half an hour depending on the guy. Once it's over, they are not interested in you. They want to get rid of you as early as possible. The same tongue that spoke eloquently of my beauty and my complexion—which is very beautiful, nice, wheatish, yellowish, flawless skin— would then want to pack me off as soon as they could once their desires were satiated.

Thai women have smaller breast sizes. They praise you for that small size. Whatever is available for them is heaven. Once they are finished, they just do not bother; they're not interested. They pay you money and ask you to leave politely. And of course, I'm also not willing to stay back. Once my money is in my hand, I am out in a jiffy. This ritual of flesh meeting flesh and hand meeting muscled organs— everything is automatic. I was getting drained many times.

Once you start something, you cannot get away from it because that's what brings you the money. Once the money starts coming in, you look at many other facilities and gadgets. You depend on them, and you cannot stay away from them. That is the reason they say that a poor man can survive even if he becomes rich, but if a rich man becomes poor, he cannot survive because he will miss those facilities. This can make him crazy and sometimes he will kill himself. Money can be a curse or a boon, depending on the circumstances.

Chapter 11

I am one who is from a village and came to a big city to seek opportunities. I sometimes feel that I am great, that I am the chosen one. My karma brought me so much happiness, so many orgasms at one go. My soulmate, my boyfriend, after a sexual encounter, would talk and discuss sex, life, philosophy, denials, so many topics. All this made me intelligent. I was listening, reading, and understanding human feelings, interactions, and the sadness of life.

I feel that sex is a subject; it was created by Mother Nature as the second hunger after the food. Everybody spends a lot of time fantasizing about it. Many dare to explore it, but the majority locks it in. The situation should change; that is where education is very much required. The society should be brave to offer the same to the generations to come so that they do not suffer or face the same tribulations that the earlier ones suffered and the present ones are suffering. I'm confident things are changing for the good. People are understanding, and slowly things will change. It will be good for the people to understand and practise and take in a lot of knowledge to enjoy their sex lives.

My boyfriend came unannounced, and I was not there. I had gone on a visit to my family at my place near Sisaket. He went to the shop at ten o'clock, and he waited for me. Then the girls started going in, and he asked one of my friends where I was.

She said, 'She has gone home. She didn't know that you were coming.'

He said, 'Yes, I had some time, so I came to meet her.'

'Don't worry, I will phone and tell her to come.'

That time we never had cell phones. There was a landline, and my friend called me and said, 'Your boyfriend has come.'

My heart was racing in anticipation of a steamy sex session. 'Wait,' I told her. 'I need a day. I have some work for my mum at the hospital. Tell him to wait. I will be there as soon as I can.' My friend conveyed the same to him.

He said, 'No problem. It's my fault. I had not informed her. I will wait.'

I came back after two days and knocked on his room. He was waiting for me. He just hugged me, kissed me, held me for ten minutes. His eyes were misty, and he was very, very happy to see me.

I told him, 'You came just like that. I didn't know. Normally, you would give me your schedule, but this time, you did not.'

He said, 'Yes, I understand. I had some spare time, and I could come, so I came. No problem.'

I asked him what he did these two days. There was a mischievous smile on my face. He said he got a foot massage, not an oil massage where he had to remove his clothing. He had a foot massage in my shop with my friend, went for a walk, visited a temple. He had food at the same place we always went into. That was it. Then he came back to the room, read a book, and slept. I'd always seen him with many books; he was a good reader. He told me that was how it was. The same pattern continued for both days.

I asked him, 'Why not take a girl?'

He was offended. He looked at me seriously and said, 'Do you want me to?'

I said, 'Well, I was not here. You could always take someone and have a good time. I want you to have a good time. I have no problem with it.'

He knew I was taunting him. I was trying to understand him. He said, 'No issues, I am not that good a man, but in Thailand, whenever I come, I will have a relationship and sex only with you and not with anyone else.'

I was touched. I was pleased. I was elated. I was very happy.

I was with him the whole day. He hugged me. He kept on talking to me. He told me many, many stories. Now I understood whatever he said to a great extent. He entered me with so much force—of course, without hurting me—and he was very happy to have a beautiful go with me. I was so happy to have a double orgasm. He went through the whole routine. We rested and watched TV for some time. We both went for a swim, then came back. We were hungry. We ordered food from the restaurant, and we both slept for some time. I woke up, and I searched for him on the bed. He was sitting on a chair and looking at me.

I said, 'What are you looking at?'

He said, 'Nothing. I was just watching you sleep like a baby. You are tired. You have been in a bus all the way, ten hours, eleven hours.'

Now we have many buses travelling directly from my village to Pattaya City, which is the most popular place in Thailand for all the tourists. So the bus owners have provided many buses as the business is good.

He called me to go near him, and I sat on his lap. He started kissing me on my back and neck, and he kept on fondling my tits. My breasts started swelling, and he kept on rubbing. He was all ready with a strong erection. I had nothing beneath my robe, and he lifted it up. He entered me from the rear into my vagina. It was sudden. He had a very strong erection, and he went up to the hilt. He started moving. I started moving. It was divine. We both continued for many minutes. We both were panting, and he stopped, got up, made me bend on the bed. I was on all my fours. Again, he entered my vagina from the rear. The walls of my vagina, which are used to certain penetrations and certain fits from certain angles, will give certain results. But for any new thing, there are untouched portions of the vagina that can give you more pleasure.

I was feeling something new happening to me. He was basically rotating clockwise and anticlockwise. It was a great feeling.

I said, 'What's happening?'

He said, 'Enjoy it. It's a new technique—a doggie. Time to implement, practise on you, would love to try to implement the new posture on you.'

'Oh, am I a lab mouse?'

'No, you are a beautiful rabbit. Don't worry, I'm not using you as an experimental thing. Let's enjoy this. Stop talking. Less talk, more action.'

He continued his pumping. Believe me, he could do it for fifteen to twenty minutes by hitting hard, slowing down, changing the rhythm, diverting, and fondling my breasts and other parts of the body, my stomach, my back, my thighs, my face, my lips, my ears, my nose, my eyes, my forehead, and all over. I was almost ready, and I told him I was ready. He said, 'I know. Relax. Hold it. Do not come.' He kept pumping, and it was a great feeling. Maybe those two days of separation after he came had given him all the zest.

The first round was faster because he was more excited; the second round was divine. He kept on pumping, and he suddenly made me turn. I was on my back on the bed, and he went into the missionary position. I suppose that is the most convenient one for everyone. He was crushing me; my breasts were flattened. He was kissing me, and he started moaning. I was moaning. Then he said, 'I am Cumming.' I said, 'I am Cumming.' And we both came. It was a great go. He kept on pumping, and I matched thrust to thrust. His semen was pouring in me, and my cum was coming out, and I had one of the greatest orgasms I would never forget.

We had such beautiful sex; it was divine. It was as delicious as good food, which satisfies your palate. Sex satisfies your mind body and maybe the soul. We were spent, and we were together for, say, maybe ten, fifteen minutes. Then he slowly and reluctantly withdrew from me. We washed and went back, holding each other, hugging. Our two bodies became one, and we both instantly fell asleep. For how many hours we slept, we did not know. It was dark. Maybe three, four hours must have passed. We got up smiling, admiring each other, and then we decided we were really hungry. We both left for a walk to catch up with our dinner.

Chapter 12

My boyfriend was very eager to spend more time with me. He suggested in one of his visits that we go out of Pattaya. In Pattaya, I was tied down to my routine. I had to report to my boss. I had to work in the shop, and I had less time to spend with him. I took the cue. I asked for a leave of absence from my boss.

She raised an eyebrow, saying, 'What? Where are you going?'

I said, 'Well, my boyfriend wants to spend more time with me. He's asking me to go on a small tour and maybe a week's holiday.'

'Okay, you've been working hard. You've gone through hell after your marriage broke down. You've been working here. You're getting a break, and you have a good boyfriend. Go have a great time.'

This was what I liked in my boss; she was also from a background similar to mine. She understood my feelings, my emotions, and my difficulties. If I could also be happy like any other person, then why not? This was what I appreciated in my boss's attitude.

I was so excited; I called my house and told my people that I was going on a tour to Krabi. The tour was within Thailand, and I didn't need a passport; my ID was good enough. The exciting thing was, I was flying down from Bangkok's Suvarnabhumi International Airport to Krabi. It's a nice place with beaches, and the huge Indian Ocean lies in front of you. So we both went to a travel agent. We worked out a plan; we bought our air tickets from Bangkok to Krabi. There are two airports in Bangkok. One is Suvarnabhumi, and the other one is Don Muang Airport; both are international ones, and they handle domestic passengers as well.

We bought our tickets, we booked our rooms, and we just went from Pattaya to Suvarnabhumi Airport; it's one hundred and twenty kilometres or so. I was all excited. It was my first flight, and I had never gone on an aeroplane. With all the excitement in my heart, I was holding his hand, and he was smiling at me. We both went into the airport, finished our check-in. It was an airline where one bag was free, but the second bag you had to pay for. We had three bags, so we had to pay for one bag. We finished the security clearance, finished all the frisking, and then we got into the escalator and went down to the departure gate.

There were a lot of people; it was a mixed crowd of all ethnic origins, Europeans, Americans, Asians, and Thais. It was like a big fish market. We always talked of the fish market because we spent more time buying fish to have a nice meal. We waited for the departure announcement, then we got into the queue. Our boarding passes were scrutinized, and a portion was given to us with our seat numbers. We climbed up the steps. This being a short domestic flight, there was no vestibule connected directly to the aircraft. So we had to climb the steps of the ladder in the tarmac to get into the plane.

I was wondering how many seats it had—three this side and three on the other side. Okay. I got a window seat. He had made sure I got a window so that I could look at the beautiful scenery from the sky. He made me wear my seatbelt. The announcements were made. The headcount was done, and the doors were closed. The air hostess explained about how to wear a seatbelt and oxygen mask, about emergencies, and about the food that would be served. It was a short flight; we were given snacks and some soft drinks and coffee or tea. The plane started moving. I was scared though I'm a brave girl. I remembered that. I held on to his hand.

He patted me, saying, 'Not to worry, everything is fine. There are so many people here like you and me. Nothing will happen.'

So it taxied down on the runway, then it picked up speed. Then the captain announced, 'In your stations for take-off.'

And soon the plane took off to the sky. It climbed up, up, up to 30,000 feet or 35,000 feet. I didn't know. When we were levelled, I was very happy seeing the clouds and scared of the small turbulences. I was totally in awe, and I was totally excited.

Life can also be like this. You can get into your plane, and you can start flying. This is the life of many, but majority of people cannot afford this kind of flying. Seeing my poor life or my background, I always compare. Why can't others also enjoy the good things in life? It's a good thing that you think about others who also should have good things in life so that later on, if you develop that ability and if you can create that kind of money, you can help hundreds of people to fly.

Right now, I wanted to enjoy what had been offered to me. We were offered snacks, juices. The captain announced our descent. There was some sort of vacuum or air pressure within the aircraft. Many were putting cotton buds in their ears. Many were holding their noses and blowing air. I had no such problem. I was just enjoying it. The plane landed beautifully without any jerks, and the plane came to a halt.

We got off the plane, collected our luggage, took a taxi, and went to our room. It was a good hotel, a three-star one. We were well received. All the reservations were organized by our travel agent, who was a good guy. We were given a good room facing the sea, and I was very, very happy. We hugged each other, held on to each other.

We were hungry, so we said, 'Let's go wash ourselves and go for a bite.' We washed ourselves, held each other, and I gave him a long passionate kiss.

He said, 'Wow, you're all excited.'

I said, 'Yes, I am excited. I'm very happy. I flew for the first time, and I'm going to fly again back to Bangkok.'

'Yes, yes, there will be many more flights to come.' These were his words, and it came true.

Later on in my life, I travelled a number of times to Kuala Lumpur in Malaysia and to many places in Thailand. We went and had a nice hot meal of rice, some pork, some fish, and a dessert in the hotel's restaurant. We went for a walk and saw so many tourists walking on the streets, all excited. We went to a local travel agent and found out the nearby sightseeing destinations.

The next day, we booked for a ride to an island called Phi Phi Island. It's one and a half to two hours one way by a ferry, a small-sized ship. It is a sought-after destination with scenic views of the Indian Ocean. We took our tickets, then went back to our room. We were sort of tired, but at the same time, we were all excited, so we quickly changed. We both agreed to take a nap, and then we'd see what we would do afterwards. There was a mischievous smile on his face and my face. We both agreed it was time to take a nap, and he kept on telling me to sleep for some time.

I kept on telling him, 'Wait, let me see how ready you are.'

'I'm always ready' was what he said, but we decided not to start anything now since we've just eaten. We would try to abstain from any sex for the time being, and slowly we both slipped off to our sleep. When we woke up, three hours had passed through just like that.

We got up from our bed, then we both decided to have a shower together. He undressed and got into the shower. I'd always liked it lukewarm, but he liked it hot. So it was a compromise—not very hot and not very cold. So we decided to have a 'blow hot and cold' shower. He took the soap solution and started slowly rubbing my back. Hot water falling on me and then the nice movement of his hand—up and down, in circles, clockwise, and then anticlockwise—were very comforting and relaxing. He started from my neck, my shoulders, my back, the small of my back, my buttocks, and then after he made me part my legs a little, my anus, my thighs, and slowly his hand was moving down to my vagina.

I told him, 'What?'

He said, 'Nothing, I'm just massaging you.'

'You want to massage my vagina?'

'Maybe, maybe not.' So he started slowly rubbing, pressing, and feeling my vagina, and his other fingers were moving behind my buttocks. It was a hot feeling, a hot feeling from inside. It was nice; he was actually taunting me. He was getting me excited. His hands kept slowly feeling the inner portions of my vagina. He was trying to figure out how to enter the opening of my vagina. He slowly put his finger in and started moving it. The feeling was good, and it was from the rear.

Any new penetration other than the penetration you are normally used to that just touches the untouched portions of the walls of your private part can excite you greatly. This is the reason they have so many postures or positions being experimented in Kama Sutra.

He was moving slowly. His other finger was rubbing my clit, and I was getting excited. I wanted to turn to hug him.

He said, 'No.'

He slowly sat down in the bathtub and started rubbing my vagina. I was getting hot, hotter, and I was trying to move.

He said, 'Do as you wish, but don't ask me to remove my fingers.'

I was saying no in my hoarse voice. He understood I was getting excited. He kept on moving. I was building up, and I think slowly I was coming. He suddenly stopped.

I said, 'Why?' I was annoyed.

He said, 'Easy, I'll make it more interesting.'

He was on his knees, and he slowly put his tongue into my private part. I was getting tickled, and it was a new experience. No one has ever done this to me before. He made me turn and made me sit on the elevated part of bathtub and made me part my legs, and he kept on using his tongue expertly on my clitoris and on the entrance of my vagina; he was going inside my vagina up and down. It was a tremendous experience, and I was getting totally excited. He kept on moving slowly, and he was nibbling at my clitoris; it was a great experience. I was getting totally high. I wanted this to go on, and he kept on the momentum. I was enjoying it immensely.

He started slowly biting my clitoris, and I was feeling a slight pain, but at the same time, it was so exhilarating; it was so enjoyable. I was slowly feeling that something was happening inside my gut. He slowly introduced a finger into my vagina and started moving, and then at the same time, he was using his tongue, which kept on nibbling and hitting my clitoris. It was a two-front attack, and the feeling was tremendous. This went on for quite some time, and I was totally spent.

And I said, 'I'm coming.'

He said, 'Go ahead, you're welcome.'

And then I burst out, and it was all wet; the water was trickling.

Then he said, 'Go ahead and enjoy.' And he increased the momentum of both his tongue and his finger inside me and outside. It was a great spent. I was totally relaxed. It was heaven on earth. And I felt I was seeing my god and seeing my creator. It's what sex can give. This is called heaven on earth or hell on earth. Whatever the name you want to give it, you can give it.

I kept on resting, relaxing, but he didn't allow me to relax. He was excited by this act. He made me sit on him, and he slowly entered my vagina; we were locked together face to face. And he started licking my breasts. They were getting his attention, and he started sucking my breasts. They were swelling, and they were wanting more affection. He was giving due care to both my breasts by sucking, pressing, and slowly fiddling with my nipples. It was a fantastic feeling. He was hugging me. He was licking me. He was sucking me. And the whole experience was great. He was hard; he had entered me for the first time in this position. And we started slowly moving. It was divine; it was beautiful.

My words are too jumbled to explain these kinds of feelings, but the real feeling is from your gut, from your heart. You'll feel very great, very nice. The guys who created all of us must have used their ingenuity in creating sex. Sex can give so much happiness to two individuals—a man and a woman, a man and a man, or a woman and a woman. What are the chemicals which react so beautifully? And it can give so much happiness during all those outings or maybe threesome or foursome or five some. I don't know, but the majority is twosome.

Two people can create great music. Two people can create that kind of harmony, a rhythm which gives great happiness and can touch the pinnacle. It's like you're seeing the whole world opening up for you, and at that moment, it is nirvana. I recall it is like being one with your god or one with your creator. This kind of happiness, this kind of rhythm will come only when two people understand, coordinate, give, take, share, and care for each other. It is a science. It is a thing to research. It has to be taught to all people in this world who are sexually not knowledgeable to enjoy this God-given happiness. This is available to them, and they can have such great fun by using their bodies and enjoying the same.

Well, back to my action. We both were hugging each other, and he was getting stronger as he started moving. I was moving; I'm a strong girl. As I felt he was tired, I started moving speedily. The speed was so great.

He said he was 'coming'.

'You welcomed me earlier, now I'm welcoming you. Go ahead and let us finish at the same time.'

I was also ready, and we both exploded into one of the greatest explosions of marital bliss of two bodies. The yin and yang or the plus and minus can create the greatest happiness when two people come together.

We were totally and happily spent, slightly tired, and then we slowly finished our shower by putting soap on each other, then we dried each other. He went back in the bedroom and lay down on the bed, and we kissed each other, hugged each other.

I said, 'Let's watch television soap.'

He said, 'No, we'll see the news. Otherwise, you will get hooked to your program, and we will miss our outing.'

We got dressed after resting for a while. We were both feeling happy; our faces were flushed. We took a walk on the main street of Krabi's downtown area. There was one main street where all the entertainment and restaurants were situated. A lot of young girls called customers for a massage in their shops, which reminded me of my job. A lot of girls were smiling, waving to the passing tourists to find their customers and spend a great day with them. They were looking for their bread and maybe a little butter, definitely not jam.

We went from one end of the road from our hotel to the other end. There was a big restaurant complex, and they had advertised an adult cultural show. We both decided to take a shot at it. We asked how much for the entrance; it was one thousand baht (Thai money). From dollar conversion, it was not much; it was around thirty US dollars. We went inside to our allotted table. They asked us what we would like to drink. We asked for some Scotch. It was a watered-down Scotch. The small one was given to us with some peanuts and some crackers to go with it.

After a few minutes, the show started. There were many adult girls dancing on the stage, scantily clad, giving out songs from hit Thai movies, and there were many boys trying to seduce those girls on the stage. It was an adult show, and all the tourists were enjoying the visuals and the singing. There was a lot of excitement. Many couples, old men, young men, old ladies were all having a good time. Then there were many jokers trying to speak in broken English, making funny lewd jokes to bring in the sex humour.

After an hour or so, one beautiful lady came on to the stage, and a well-muscled man also joined in. They started dancing; they both were experts in dancing. They started peeling off their clothes one by one, and then they were totally naked. The man had a nicely shaved pubic area and a penis that was maybe six, seven inches long. He was aroused, or maybe he was given an injection to make him get a big erection. I was told this is what was done for the guys who had to have sex on the stage for a prolonged period. The lady had big breasts, not very normal to a Thai lady. She must have been chosen for that reason to do the show. They both started hugging each other, kissing each other, feeling each other. She was making a lot of actions. It was erotic; at the same time, it was sexual. They were trained to make others feel the excitement of whatever they were depicting.

The lady took the man's penis. She started sucking it. Later, the man made the woman lie down, and he started using his tongue on her vagina. A little later, he entered the lady from the front, back, side—a lot of acrobatic postures that was possible only for those who had a body well trained or well prepared to do such acts. They did five, six, seven, or eight different postures each time. He was entering and maintaining the erection and moving in her for four minutes to five minutes; it was almost more than forty-five minutes. How could the man hold on? Maybe he was a superman or he had been prepared or trained to control his mind.

He kept on moving in her, and then things were getting all excited that people were also moving in their seats. There were many couples hugging each other, and their hands were busy on each other. We both were smiling, holding our hands, and maybe we kissed once or twice; we were also getting excited. But we had just finished our session and were spent. The man and the woman finally reached a stage when he took out his penis from her vagina, and then he put his penis in her hand. She kept it near her breasts and started moving it on all directions. He was panting; she was all excited. She held it in her mouth for a few minutes. She was making a lot of movements, then he was also getting excited. Finally, she kept it between her breasts and started moving it, then he ejaculated. The hot semen hit her on her chin, face, mouth, all over her breasts. He kept on moving slowly, and he again entered her vagina and started lifting her off her feet. He made her put her legs behind his back, and he was pumping in furiously with an equal response from his partner. They finished with a lot of loud erotic sounds.

It was a great feat for a man to perform. It was fantastic. It was out of the world. It was unique. It was awesome. Whatever words you can use, you can say. Everybody was clapping and shouting, 'Hooray!' All were very pleased. After that, the lady and the man rushed out after bowing to the audience.

We were told the show was over. We got up, but to our surprise, we saw the man and the woman both dressed and shaking hands with all of us and a tip box was kept at the exit. We were happy to tip them for their great act.

We shook their hands and said, 'Well done.'

They thanked us and said, 'Come once again.'

We said, 'Thank you. Sure.'

Civility costs nothing; we have to be polite with people. We said bye, and then we both came out. We were hungry after the watered-down whiskey, the small one. We went to a Thai restaurant, had one more shot of whiskey, and we ordered some prawn fry, fish curry, and rice. We ate fast and hungrily to fill our stomachs and finished our drinks.

Thais do not like to eat dessert; we don't like sweets. But my boyfriend likes it, so we ordered mango, sticky rice, and sweetened thick coconut milk, which was very tasty. Then hand in hand, we walked back to our hotel room. It was a beautiful experience. We both went into the room. It was very cool inside. A hot or mild shower will give you a good sleep as we all sweated it out in the hot climate outside. A beach town is warm, and you sweat a lot; that is the goodness of the climate. In an air-conditioned atmosphere, you feel that chillness; that is how life is made—hot and cold.

We finished our shower, went back, and we both sat on the bed, looking at each other intently. I knew what was going to happen. He was just looking at me.

I asked him, 'What is that look? You want to have sex?'

He said, 'No, no, I was just looking at your beauty.'

'Come on, cut the crap. I know exactly what you are looking at. You want to have a go. You have to have sex as the boy and girl were having on the stage. They are in their twenties. They can be acrobatic, and we cannot be what they are.'

Then he said, 'Absolutely not, we can do only certain postures, maximum maybe twenty, but those guys can do even sixty-nine if they are taught how it can be done.'

I asked him, 'Do you know all the sixty-nine postures?'

'Yes, theoretically but, practically, only twenty at this age. When I was young, I could do another thirteen or fourteen more.'

I told him not to brag about his ability to perform. 'Now what should we do?'

'We will sleep. We have eaten. We have to relax.' He told me, 'After consuming food, you should have at least a three-hour gap before you indulge in any active physical activity. More or less, this points to sex.'

I asked, 'What will happen if we have sex immediately after eating?'

'You can, but you might have indigestion, stomach problems, and then you cannot enjoy it for the next two or three days. Prevention is better than cure.'

Then I said, 'Okay, let us go to sleep.'

He said thank you, and then he went to sleep. In five minutes, he was off.

I could not get any sleep because I slept in the afternoon, so I watched a TV program. A nice Thai movie was showing, and I enjoyed seeing the problems a young girl had to face in life and what she had to do to manage her life and her family. All over the world, I suppose they depict the difficulties undergone by a woman. The idea is not that they are very much interested in the difficulties of a woman but that, whatever the process she goes through and whatever she does, they will show her body (semi-naked, little naked, or more naked) and her beautiful face through her suffering. It is so women-oriented; 90 per cent of movies show women. In most advertisements, they show women, and in every kind of promotion, women are shown as the great attraction provider or destroyer and, at the same time, fun giver.

When I finished the movie, I also thought I would sleep, then I saw him sleeping nicely. I slipped out of my dress, and I got into the bed with him. I was not feeling sleepy; maybe I was excited after seeing that show, and I rarely got sex of this kind of total penetration, total romance with the good body of my boyfriend. I did carry out many mechanical massages, many mechanical happy endings, and, maybe if the money was good, some sexual activity with my customers. But they were all done purely from the money point of view. I did it sincerely for the sake of money, not for the sake of myself. The mind is the greatest player, and it decides what is good for you. One person's food is another person's poison. My mind, my mind-set, my circumstances, my life had brought me to a situation where I did a job which involves my body. I did it for the sake of making money, but now, when I was totally relaxed and rested after enjoying good food and a nice show, I was getting excited.

I slowly started going near him, held him from his back. I slowly moved my whole body to adjust to his posture and slept like that for five minutes. He was a light sleeper, but that day, the journey, the afternoon sex, the show, good food, and that kind of physical activity must have tired him. He did not move. I made him lie down on his back, and I removed the blanket and started kissing him from his toe to his foot, ankle, and knees and slowly went up to his chest. I got on him, and he suddenly woke up and got me into focus. He was all smiles, and he was half-asleep.

I said, 'Do not make any sound. Go to sleep, relax. Let me work.'

He said, 'Okay, fine.'

I started kissing him. He responded, his tongue moving in my mouth; there was a 'sword fight' going on. We were locked together. Then I kissed him on his cheeks, chin, neck, and nipples, and slowly I moved down to his already hardened penis. It's a majestic and magnificent tool with a length of seven to eight inches. It is much longer than the ones I have seen. I started teasing him. He was still. I started moving my mouth on it and started sucking it slowly and nibbling on it and moving it up and down. He was totally up.

He said, 'It's very nice.'

I said, 'Yes, definitely. It would be nice if you enjoyed it. You deserve it.' I started playing on his two balls, the ping-pong balls that created a moment of fascination.

He said, 'I am ready.'

I said, 'Not now. Relax.'

I removed my mouth from his organ and started using my mouth on his testicles, and then I was feeling his inner thigh; I was trying to find his 'G spot'. You know, everybody—man or woman—has a G spot. The spot for the man is between the anus point and the point between the two testicles. I started using my tongue, and he was virtually wriggling.

He was asking me to go on top of him and let him enter me. I asked him not to hurry but to wait. He kept on requesting, and I thought I would liberate him. I went back, put his penis in my mouth, and started moving up and down. My mouth became the vagina. He was totally excited, and he was almost trying to dislodge me.

I said, 'Relax,' and then I started moving in a faster pace, then he was about to explode in my mouth. Immediately, I removed it, I put his penis in my vagina, and his penis was totally inside me. He started moving, then he made me turn and lie down on the bed. He was on top of me, and he started pumping up and down. It was very surprising, that kind of stamina. He was almost an old man, touching maybe his sixties. He kept on going for some time.

I said, 'Do no stop.'

He said, 'I will do my best.'

He kept on hitting me hard, then we both exploded, and he was totally spent. He was all excited and flushed up, so relaxed. He kept on thanking me for the great treat I provided him.

I said, 'It was my pleasure. You are a good man. You deserve the best.'

He said, 'You are a good girl.'

He calls me the sexy lady of Thailand, and I call him a sexy, worldly man. All the fun and jokes aside, I kept on thinking how one could enjoy so much. We had two rounds. It was okay, and I felt that day was a day of total happiness. It was like I had seen heaven, and this is the time you feel you are one with the power which created us. This is the total happiness a person can get. What more is required? We can be one with the power in total peace and harmony; this you cannot get through anything else other than the meeting of two bodies which produces such great sex.

We came down from heaven to earth, had a wash, hugged each other, went back, and lay down wrapped in each other's arms. Believe me, you do get great sleep after good sex, especially if you had an orgasm. Men finish fast. Women take time, and in this world, there are so many women who sleep on their back with eyes open, totally not satisfied. They are unsatisfied, and their husbands next to them are in deep sleep, maybe sometimes snoring. They just finish fast and furious because that is how a man's body is made. Of course, there are many men who cannot perform due to various reasons, like too much alcohol, stress, worries, etc.

Do you know that an old man can also give a lot of happiness to a woman? In spite of his half erection, in spite of him not getting the semen out of his penis, and for that matter, even if he does not get an erection, still he can have beautiful sex with his partner and make the lady totally cum. It is an art to be learned by patience and practice. This requires knowledge, training, dedication, and the will to perform. The man should not be selfish. 'I cannot do it', 'I cannot get my semen out' should be taken out of his mind. You have a moral duty to your partner to make her cum if she is excited. You start well, but you cannot perform, then you withdraw, and you find ways to make her cum even if you cannot—no issues. The body is not producing that action. We will work on that to make you cum. There are many things you can do to improve your bodily functions. Let us set that aside.

Going back to the women who lie down on the bed, unsatisfied and dreaming of getting an orgasm, I have read somewhere there are many women who do not know that they can also get an orgasm. Many ladies have lived with their husbands for twenty, thirty, or forty years—mostly in Asian countries or maybe all over the world—without knowing that they too can get an orgasm. But the ladies can definitely demand an orgasm from their partners. It is possible for a man who underperforms to make the lady get that total satisfaction.

My boyfriend hugged me, held on to me, then he said, 'I am very happy. I am going to sleep. Let me sleep.' He was already asleep earlier.

I said, 'Go ahead, sleep.'

I tucked him in, put an extra pillow next to him, and told him to sleep, and in few minutes, he was totally asleep. He was at peace with himself. I was on my back, cosy while lying down, a smile on my face. I was happy outside and inside, and I was just trying to understand the mysteries of life.

Persons are born as a child, grow up, become a teen, and then they are aware of their sexuality. I think it is at this age that they are eager to have sex. The mysteries of sex are unfolded in the four walls of their lives. I am unable to decipher who created all this, who made all this. Let us assume for a minute there was no sex between a man and a woman or between two people. Then you are born, you grow, and you die. How we are brought on to earth? By whom? By the sex energy. How do you get this energy? It is the chemicals produced by the body by food consumption, which in turn converts to semen, and a child is formed and born when it mates with the egg of a female. But all the mysteries, who did all these?

Sometimes I think I am not a well-educated lady. I only had schooling for ten years, but of course, there are many with no schooling at all in this world. I was chosen. I have been drafted by the power or by nature or by existence to do something different in my life.

I am a beautiful lady. I started laughing out loudly. Then suddenly, I stopped to look at my guy; he was in his heaven. I remembered he told me that when everybody sleeps, their souls keep some kind of point of recognition near the body and go out on outings. He had explained to me earlier that we have three stages in our mundane lives. One is wakefulness; that is when you are awake. You know what is happening to you. You know what is going on in front of you. You can see, hear, smell, touch, and feel. But when you go to sleep and you dream, it is the second stage, the dream stage. Sometimes it is about the day's happenings. Sometimes it is from your subconscious, which has absolutely no connection with what has happened to you in your life. Maybe something terrible happening to you can be there in your dreams. The dream has two sub stages—that is, the surface level and deep-sleep level. But the deep-sleep level is the third stage. When you are deeply asleep, the soul or the atman leaves the body and keeps a point of recognition near your body for it to come back, and then it goes on its errand. We do not know where it goes. No one knows. No researcher has come up with an answer to this. It goes, and whether it goes to meet the existence, the creator, the god, we do not know—or to meet its boyfriend or girlfriend, no one knows.

Elders say that when a person is asleep, you should slowly wake up the person who is in their sleep. Slowly call, touch them. It should not be sudden because the soul has to come back from wherever it has gone and enter the body so that it can make the body open its eyes and go to the wakeful stage.

So I was just wondering, *My guy is totally asleep, where has his soul gone roaming?*

People say that beauty is skin-deep, but the whole world is gaga about beauty. No one wants to look at any ugly thing. No one wants to look at difficulties; they just brush it aside. Everyone wants a nice, beautiful female or male body that's nicely contoured and attractive for the body and the mind; that is what is aspired.

I was sent to work as a maid to Bangkok. They are also not bad memories. I could see the great city of Bangkok. I could see the life of the rich and famous. I worked hard and took care of a child and understood how dependent a child can be. My four years in the house of a rich guy in Bangkok taught me a lot of neatness, a lot of discipline and gave me the vision to be somebody important in life. It gave me the impetus to become rich, for me to have a good lifestyle.

This kind of motivation is what is happening today. TV is a common factor for everybody, whether you are super-rich or slum poor. Everybody watches TV. All the serials, advertisements, dramas, movies—majority show palatial houses with great big gardens. All boys, girls, men, and women are dressed neatly in expensive clothes and move in expensive cars. Life is shown as a great entertainment. We enjoy the entertainment value, but we forget in the process to sow the seeds of hope, that we should also grow to be like others, which will drive us to achieve that target.

This drive to achieve makes the majority to adopt shortcuts. As we all know, we're all born equals to be unequal. The children from affluent families can get excellent education. They achieve their targets to become doctors, engineers, architects, scientists, diplomats, and they do succeed. They're all smart kids; they are trained and inculcate the art to acquire all the knowledge required to be a successful person. When it comes to the majority of the poor, their economic status decides their lifestyle. But a minority—I would call it a minuscule minority—do achieve, do go up by studying in ordinary schools. They are extraordinary guys, but the majority ends up as dropouts.

When they attempt, they manage to finish schooling up to the tenth. Then they find ways and means as they are driven by their poverty to find a job. They become mechanics, and they become electricians, doing odd jobs. There is a lot of demand for air conditioner mechanics to work in the big cities, so they take mediocre jobs, and they try to achieve or excel in their chosen fields. Maybe they're highly intelligent guys that they're able to excel in their work, but the scope for them to make money is limited because of their jobs. Whatever they do entitles them to only a certain amount of money. They can't get the salary of an engineer. They can't get the salary of a doctor if they're a compounder or a nurse.

So this kind of comparison goes on, but children of the same age, the boys or the girls, are exposed to the same kind of situations in the society. Some aspire to live in a big house. They can't because they don't have the funds, whereas a guy with the money can command it as he already has it.

Whatever he acquires extra is savings for him. The majority of the poor accepts the inculcation done to them from their very young age as their karma. 'We are supposed to be this.' 'We are suppose to live like this.' That's it. 'We can't aspire for bigger things because we were not chosen.' It's technically not very acceptable to the boy or the girl, but they have no choice, so they understand the situation.

That's where the inculcation, the surroundings, their upbringing comes into play. They believe in fate, destiny, or karma, and they settle down because their bodily juices or chemicals work and there are basic issues they are more interested in. They find their own slots at their own level for getting a boy or a girl, and they try to settle down and build a family. This is a vicious cycle, It goes on to produce a lot of mediocre guys, super-intelligent guys, rich guys, poor guys, and ordinary guys. Everybody is made in terms of the karma they have, not by their intelligence, not by their capacity. These are all set aside. They continue the work they are destined to do, live, and rejoice.

Going back to a small minority of guys who are frustrated and want to achieve big, they see in TV a guy who is a young fellow going in beautiful cars, living in great houses, zooming around in nice bikes, going in planes, and they want to achieved that kind of lifestyle. A small portion does succeed in finding great jobs by breaking that barrier of a tough line between the rich and the poor and getting into that rich bracket.

Then there is a portion of guys who adopt shortcuts. They become criminals. They become breakers of the law. See the tough line. There are many super-rich guys who break the law every day, but by using their intelligence, they manipulate it and are not caught. But if a guy who has no background breaks the law, he's caught, and he ends up in jail. There are a number of instances like this.

I was reading in the paper that two boys who wanted quick money saw an old man. They followed him to his big house. They watched the house for some time. He was living alone. His family, everybody, was abroad. So they went to the house, ringing the bell on some pretext. They killed the guy, took away whatever money was there, and took also the credit card of that man. They had a great life for a week or ten days from the money they had taken from the old man by going to great restaurants and going to many entertainment spots. After that, they wanted more money because they had tasted the pleasure money can buy. They didn't know how to use the credit card properly. They didn't want to buy anything with it because it was of no use to them; they wanted the cash. So they came up with a great idea. They went into a petrol bunk; they had negotiated earlier with another guy that they would give him 100 litres of diesel. They wanted to swipe the credit card for 100 litres of diesel. The petrol guys became suspicious. They called the police, the guys were caught, and they went through the process of law. This is just an example. There are thousands and thousands of different cases of guys with no knowledge of robbing and no knowledge to become rich trying to do it and ending up in jail. The feeling, the urge to become rich, the longing to make more money and enjoy the goodies in life can drive a minority of guys to adopt shortcuts.

Well, I went to so many places in my thoughts—working for a rich guy. The differences between the rich and the poor—all these happen beyond our control. Why it happens, no one knows. Whatever happens will happen—que sera sera. Let's hope for the good. Let's have faith in the universe.

Let's have faith in godliness. Let's have faith in the power that has created us to be on this earth. This kind of wisdom should dawn on each and every mind. There are a lot of angry young men and women today in this world who feel that a lot of injustice is being done. They are hit below their belts. They take the hits straight and on the targets. They're unable to do anything. It is the duty of our society to bring in a semblance of sanity to make the haves realize and share a part of their wealth in providing shelter, clothing, food, and a bit entertainment. I hope things will fall into place. Let's have all the faith in the universe to show its charisma.

I returned back from my thoughts. I was lying on the bed; my eyes were heavy with all those philosophical thoughts on the true facts of life. It's up to you all to decide whether it is useful to improve our lives. I went to the restroom, came back, turned on the other side of the bed. My guy was asleep, and he was in total peace. I closed my eyes, and I hoped my soul would travel to meet the soul of my boyfriend wherever it was and that they both would have a good time together.

What a thought. I was about to burst out laughing, but I controlled my laughter. I smiled to myself, and I fell asleep.

Chapter 13

The next morning, we were up by seven o'clock and kissed each other good morning and good day. We took quick showers separately. Normally, I took a shower first, so I could take more time to put make-up on my face, whereas he would just take a shower and not apply any talcum powder on his face. Maybe he's more manly for not applying any kind of cologne, powder, or cream. Men have their own body odour, and my man smelled good. I loved his body odour. So we were ready by eight in the morning. We both rushed to the restaurant for our complimentary breakfast. We had some juices. He had some cornflakes, and I had some rice, fish, and pork. I love sausages and ham. He ate a lot of fruits, toasts, and two egg omelettes without the yellow yoke in it. He takes tea most of the time and coffee once in a while. I don't drink coffee or tea.

We finished our breakfast in half an hour. We were supposed to report to the travel agent at nine o'clock for our trip to Phi Phi Island. At nine o'clock, we were at the travel agency office, which was just two, three buildings away from our hotel; we were all taken in a van. There was a ferry waiting for us, and we got into it. We were all given life jackets to wear, and we were ushered into a big hall where there were around two hundred people accommodated in an air-conditioned room for our journey. There were shops selling soft drinks and short eats on the first floor of the ferry.

At the right time, the ferry took off towards Phi Phi Island. We were on the deck, hand in hand, hugging each other, and kissing each other. There were many couples doing the same; all were eager to savour the movement.

The boat entered the middle of the Indian Ocean; all around, for 360 degrees, there was water, water, and water. After some time, we went through certain stone formations in the ocean, the nature-created wonders in the water. At one point in time, we were told to look at a particular point where we could see many dolphins jumping out of the water. It was a rare sight; we all enjoyed looking at it. We could see many fishes all playing with their families, groups, grandfathers, grandmothers, fathers, mothers, uncles, aunties, sons, daughters, children, grandchildren, great-grandchildren. What beautiful communities living in the ocean. We all grab them for our food. Who is going to grab us for their food? Maybe there is somebody waiting . . .

In our journey to Phi Phi Island, we had two stops on the way out. There was a huge hollow space in a very big cave where our ferry passed. We could look at a lot of darkened areas, and we could see light coming through one big opening from the rooftop. There were many stones, which were all eroded. The ones at the bottom had taken different shapes and colours by the water hitting it every now and then in high tide. They were maybe at a height of four, five feet, and they were a mixture of beautiful colours.

Our boat passed through a dark tunnel from this end to the other end. In the middle, there was a canopy, where more stones were looking at the sky. Great work. Which architect created this? We were asked to get down from the boat through a ladder; the distance was of maybe ten feet. We were to walk in that small area where there were a lot of small caves that led to deeper parts. All were eager to get down. We were all given flashlights, and we all walked. They suggested, 'If you guys want to swim, go ahead and swim. We'll be halting for thirty minutes.' But they also mentioned that our second stop was going to be a very beautiful place, a small island in the ocean where we could have a great swim, so it was up to us. So we thought and opted for the second destination.

We walked along, explored those small openings in the cave. It was exciting but, at the same time, a bit scary. We walked and spent some time, and thirty minutes just passed like that. We were all asked to go back to the ferry. We climbed back up the steps. It was almost a vertical climb, but no issues, we both could do it easily. The majority of the crowd that was there did attempt to climb down. There were some who were scared and did not attempt to do so, but they were all shaking their hands and encouraging us to go ahead and have fun.

Our second stop was at a very scenic, very beautiful small island. Only a trained eye could locate that speck of island in the waters of the big Indian Ocean. It was in a corner, and a small detour led us to that particular island. The boat was anchored, and we were told, 'You will have half an hour. Have a nice swim.' After the same steps of ten feet down, we just dropped into the water. There was no other facility wherein we could just walk into the island ground. Here, we had to get into the water and swim and walk to the island. It was maybe five hundred feet away; it was not very deep at that point, so we both got into the water. We kept our personal belongings in a locker in the boat, and the key was secured by me at a very safe place. Then we started swimming slowly and reached that island. The water was ice cold, and we were told the depth was hundreds of feet down on the other side—it was an ocean, not a sea. We both were trained swimmers, and there was no issue.

There were many shops selling corals, seashells. A lot of nice necklaces made out of seashells and a lot of varieties were on display. There were shops with food and drinks. From out of nowhere in the middle of the ocean, on a very small island, there were people doing business. I could see the ingenuity, see the hard work the people put in to make money, and of course, for a tourist, it was a great facility. I was proud that Thais were working very hard to make money and to serve the people.

We went around the small island; there was hardly anything there. There were a few houses where the shopkeepers lived. They were getting their supplies from the nearby little or bigger islands or maybe from Phi Phi Island. So they told us, 'We have a lot of boathouses, and many of our guys work in a similar trade. They come back in the evening, and we have no issues. We are totally protected. We move out when the sea is very rough.' Look at the adventure, look at the entrepreneurial skills they have.

In our half hour, twenty minutes had been spent, and another ten minutes were left. The guide told us, 'Come back to the ferry.' We swam back to the ferry, and when we were on board, we took a shower because we were all sticky with the seawater. We dressed, took our belongings, and sat back to continued our journey to Phi Phi Island.

Seawater is so good for your body. If you take a bath in it, it helps you to be more youthful and happier. Any positive activity will bring in a lot of cheer, and your body will react positively. We had a lot of music, songs, and happiness; a celebration was going on in the ferry, and the tourists were all having a good time.

We had some soft drinks, and after about one and a half hour, one hour and forty-five minutes, we were approaching Phi Phi Island. There was a huge tract of greenery. A lot of people on boats were visible. There were many shops that were medium-sized and some smaller ones. There were smaller boats with only five or six people travelling. They must be rich tourists who came in their own boats with all the facilities. So we reached the jetty, the ropes were thrown out, and our ferry was pulled in by the guys taking care of them. We were all told that we had three hours to spend in the island. Lunch was provided, and we were asked to go to a particular restaurant in the island. We were all hungry as usual after the trip. We walked hand in hand along with many other people. There were many friendly guys saying hi, and we were saying hi, but each one was minding their own work; all were involved with themselves. We too were doing the same.

So we walked for ten, fifteen minutes. There were many nice restaurants on the way. We went into a big place where there were already hundreds of people having their buffet lunch. We were given our tickets, and we were told to go into the huge hall which was open on all four sides. It had a nice big roof. We took our plates, our spoons, our napkins and started collecting our food. There were all varieties of food available. There was fish, pork, prawns, beef, chicken, and each one had their favourite dish. There were plenty of noodles, rice, fruits, Thai sweets, coffee, tea. Everything was available; it was a very good fare. We took what we wanted, all the food we could eat in quick time.

Hunger is a great achiever in life. You don't waste any food, and of course, if you're not hungry, you can't take a morsel of rice. It also can happen for those who are not able to eat due to their health. We had our stomachs full, and my man had a nice cup of green tea. We went to explore the island. It was a very small island; there were a few hotels where you could even stay for the night. There were many guys who came along with us from the ferry and had come with their luggage, so they had decided to stay there for a day or two and wanted to move on to some other place later. Of course, we had not known, and we had not planned for it, so we looked around. Many were fishing, many were swimming, and many were listening to music. There were a lot of celebrations; everybody was happy. I suppose life is nothing but a great celebration; people are supposed to be happy and have a real good time, and that's what life is all about.

So after three hours, we bought some raw mangoes, fruits for the return journey. The ferry took the same route but did not stop at the two points where we had stopovers on our way in. We were back in Krabi, we were transferred to a van, and we were dropped off near the travel agent's office. It was a nice and a good journey to Phi Phi Island. We were tired and went back to our room. It was almost five in the evening, and we had a wash and just slept soundly.

When we got up, it was around eight o'clock in the night. We had slept almost three hours. There is a saying that if you sleep for two hours plus at one stretch, your body will get relaxed. It is very true. We were up, and we took a shower together silently. There were body reactions. My nipples were taut, and his penis was erect, but we didn't give any attention to them. We told them, 'Please relax and wait. We are hungry to fill our stomachs, and then we shall attend to you guys to make you guys happy.' I always say that the first hunger is food, the second hunger is sex, and that they both ought to be satisfied. We had a nice shower—hot water and then cold water—and it was really refreshing and relaxing. We dressed, and we went out.

We normally didn't eat in the hotel restaurant because it had similar food to what we eat for breakfast. And again, it was more expensive. We could always try out new joints where we could have a different fare. Local delicacies were sold, and it was more exciting. We went for a walk. We were already familiar with that long street with many, many shops. The continental food, Chinese food, Indian food, Cambodian food, and Issan food were similar and spicy. Originally, in the earlier days, the whole of Thailand, Cambodia, and Laos were one, and they were called Siam. Later on, due to ethnic and minor cultural reasons, everybody parted, and Thailand now has a border with Cambodia and Laos.

I suggested that we could go to the Cambodian restaurant. Then my boyfriend said, 'Cambodian food? Yes, fine, but don't serve me fried scorpions or the other exotic dishes you like.'

'Don't worry, I will eat them, but you don't have to bother. I won't give you what you don't like.'

So we went into the restaurant. Traditional Kampuchean music was being played live. It's similar to Thai music. They don't have many differences. They're almost the same. I understand Cambodian language because they speak more of the Issan language.

We ordered some green fish curry, which contained a lot of ginger, garlic, coconut milk, and a lot of herbs. It's very exotic and very spicy, but when you add coconut milk, it tones down the spice in the curry. There is an art involved in extracting coconut milk. The grated coconut is put in boiling water and allowed to settle down. There are three types of extraction;

the first one is thicker, the second one is the middle order, and the final one is watery. So it's a combination of coconut milk and all exotic spices. It's a very nice dish.

We ordered some barbecued shrimps with rice. It was really hot and spicy. My guy also loved spicy food. We were really hungry and started eating greedily. The rice was given in small portions, but we could always opt for one more bowl. It was only twenty baht or thirty baht; that's a dollar. The gravy was spicy; it went well with the rice. The other dry dish was mushrooms with lots of herbs, cashews, onions, ginger, and of course, garlic. It was fantastic; we had such a beautiful fare.

The food was nice, and the music. Many Europeans were there. They were all dancing to this slow and melodious music. There was a Cambodian girl singing traditional songs. She was eighteen and was beautiful. The story was of kings and queens. Their adventures and their love songs were sung. It was a tremendous experience to see all this kind of live entertainment being presented at a restaurant. We were hearing many Europeans saying that they were totally bowled over by the soothing music. They are used to very little spice in their food. We locals ask to make it spicier, and they comply and give you that kind of food.

Again, we had the sweet-tooth man. My guy wanted a Cambodian sweet made out of coconut and palm sugar added to rice flour; it was more like a jelly. It was very tasty with very little sweetness in it. We enjoyed the food, the ambiance, the music, the people, and it was soothing and relaxing. We finished our food, paid the bill, tipped the waiter, and put some money in the tip box for the musicians.

There were many young guys from the West playing on their guitars near the beach, and they were singing songs, smoking, and drinking. The cops normally keep their distance from the tourists unless and until there is a problem. Generally, the cops are not visible to your eyes as there are many guys without uniform going around to protect the gullible tourists. Five fingers are not the same. Wherever there is good, there is bad. Wherever there is bad, there's ugly. Wherever there is ugly, there may be divine intervention. So it's a matter of the situation, the circumstances, and that's how life moves.

We slowly walked back towards our hotel. We were again asked by many girls to avail of a massage. They were saying, 'Come for a foot massage. You must be very tired.' That was what they called out to us. We stopped at a place, a nice small place. There were some eight, nine, ten girls all waiting for a customer. Of course, there were four, five guys inside getting their feet massaged. So we said okay. One hour was two hundred baht; that was around seven US dollars. We sat down, and we were chatting with those girls. They were all young, twenty, thirty, forty.

We could choose any one of those girls to do our massage, but I, being in the trade, asked, 'Whose turn is it?'

There was a forty-year-old lady; it was her turn. And there was another one who was thirty.

I asked him, 'Whom do you want?'

He said, 'Whomsoever you give me. It's fine for the massage.'

I suggested that he take the thirty-year-old girl to do his foot massage. The foot massage is to your foot, to your ankle, and up to your knee. So we were taken into the big room. There were nice recliners, flexible ones, and we were made to sit on them before we were stretched. They brought in warm water, washed our feet, soaked them. They took a small brush and brushed them up with soap to remove any dust particles in our legs, and they allowed our feet to soak in the warm water for some time. A few minutes later, they were taken out. They were nicely dried, and they asked us to relax. We were stretched out, and they give us small blankets to cover ourselves with if we felt cool in the air-conditioned room.

The lady asked me to relax; she took a little bit of cream and started slowly rubbing it on to my foot and on to my ankle. Then she put a nice towel to wrap it up, and then she took my other leg. She did the same thing of applying cream and started slowly pressing each finger of my leg. I told the girl in Thai to apply some pain balm to my boyfriend's legs. He had pain in his legs. But I didn't ask that for me. I knew his needs and the support he required.

I would massage him sometimes when he had pain in his legs or in his body, but he said, 'Your hands are very strong, and you don't do it slowly. You're very tough.'

I said, 'Not so, my customers are happy with me.'

'Yeah, but in your case, I feel very uncomfortable.'

'I think you dream only of sex.'

He said, 'Okay, you need not massage me. I do think of sex.'

So I told this girl to apply some pain balm to his tired legs, and she smiled and nodded. He understood what I was saying and smiled back at me. My massage lady also applied some Tiger balm and was systematically feeling each nerve in my body, from the sole of my foot. Maybe the soul of my heart was also being nicely rubbed. I was relaxing, he was relaxing, and the lady was busy in pressing and kneading, using her 'magic wand'.

All of us in the massage industry use for the foot massage a small stick of maybe four, five inches and rounded off with a grip at the bottom. We press the finer points of the toes and the sole of the foot; it's foot reflexology. Anyone can see on the Internet that there are many nerves which need soothing. Pressing them properly can give a lot of relaxation to the whole body. It is said to keep your foot or both feet in good condition and that will make your whole body relaxed, to produce positive energy. Your feet are your weightlifters. Your feet take care of the whole body weight, and they take you to many places. The feet are your passport for wonderful travel; they would expect to be maintained well.

The girls were busy for ten minutes. It was the maximum time my guy kept quiet. He started a conversation with them, and the girls asked him questions. 'Where are you from?' 'Is it okay?' 'Is it hard?' 'You want it stronger, or you want it softer?' 'How is your pain now? Is it gone?' And he asked about them, where they're from, and which part of Krabi.

Fifty per cent of the girls were from my place in the northeast. People from Chiang Mai, Chiang Rai are very beautiful; from all hill stations, all are beautiful girls, very fair, milky white, and the climate helps them maintain their natural beauty. Any hospitality trade wants or chooses good-looking girls.

The lady who was massaging me had the same sob story that I had. The lonely lady, my lady, was forty. She was from my area. She had been married, but her husband left. Two of her children were grown up and married, and she had two grandchildren. Look at that. At the age of forty, most Thai ladies (that includes me) have two, three grandchildren. As I said, we marry early, we have children early, and I suppose, we don't know what to do when we're forty. We pick up all odd jobs to survive—the same sob stories.

My boyfriend's girl spoke a little English; that was the reason I assigned her to him. She was saying she was very happy for a change. Her boyfriend was working in a hotel there. They came from Phuket; that was one of the prime tourist destinations for all the go-getters. It's a very lively place; a lot of tourists visit this beach city. In Phuket, a lot of Westerners live there for twenty, thirty years. They join as volunteers in the police force of Phuket, and they do a lot of service for the tourists who go there. They speak many languages, Western European languages or Eastern European languages, and they're doing a lot of good things for the tourists. They're all known as the tourist police.

This girl came from Phuket with her husband to make a living in Krabi. Everybody migrates. They think they can make more money in a strange place. It is because of the information which they get from somebody, and then they try to reach the place. You call that as each one's destination chosen by the power or the guy who runs the show. Whether he is a male or a female, no one knows; maybe he's transgender. We worship and bow our heads, asking the power to give us a good life, to make us happier.

So this lady from Phuket was good-looking, very polite; she was full of dreams.

She said, 'My husband, who works in a hotel, is a good cook, and one day, we hope to have a small restaurant where my husband will cook and I'll serve to make money.'

I asked, 'How about children?'

They were an exception; they had not had any children. They were postponing it. They'd picked up the idea that they would work to make money, settle down, and then raise a family. The concept is good. If you have children, you're tied down; you get responsibility. You can't move out.

The responsibility is created by us. I had my responsibility towards my two children. I had to take care of them; it was my duty. I couldn't allow them to go just like that, as orphans.

So we appreciated the forty-year-old lady and the thirty-year-old lady when they completed the massage. One hour passed, and both our legs were treated; the pain was gone for both of us. Then we were given a nice small hand massage and a neck massage—just part of the massage service—and finally, they gave us three pats on our shoulders.

And they said, 'That's it. Thank you. Wake up.'

So I said, 'Kha pun kha.'

He said, 'Kha pun khap.' Thank you.

These are the female and male versions in Thai for *thank you*.

We paid the cashier four hundred baht, and we gave one hundred baht each as tips. They were very happy. They folded both their hands and bowed down to us and said, 'Come again.' They offered us some tea, but we told them that we just had our dinner. We went out of the massage shop in better moods; our bodies were lighter compared to when we had the strain of the long journey to Phi Phi Island. We walked back to our room, said hi to the receptionist, took our keys, went to the room, changed, and got into bed. It was our second night.

We never had time for sex; we never even thought of it, to be honest, only when we were taking a shower at eight o'clock. We told them to wait, and the waiting—I think—was well worth it. They were sure to get their treat and rewards.

We settled down on the bed, and there was a knock on the door. I wondered who that was. My guy went to open the door.

I saw the receptionist, who said, 'Hi, sir.'

My boyfriend said, 'Hi, man. How are you?'

And then the receptionist gave him a CD. My guy asked him to wait for him, and he took out some money and gave it to him.

He said, 'Bye, have a good night.'

'Same to you.'

And the guy went away. I was looking at him quizzically.

He told me, 'It is nothing.'

I asked him, 'What are you up to?'

He said, 'After seeing the CD player in the room, along with the TV, I thought of getting an adult-content movie cassette.'

I said, 'Why do you want to see a movie? You don't want to sleep?'

'No, no. Just as we are on a holiday, I thought we should have more fun. Yes, now we had a massage, we're all relaxed. Until we go to sleep, why don't we look at it?'

And he said it was a Thai movie. I was interested. It was actually a very-well-made movie of two lovers who loved each other but, due to circumstances, had to part. The guy had to go away to make money, and the lady had to work to make a living. Finally, the guy went home with another lady, and this lady was waiting for him all the time. In the process, their sexual episodes and blah-blahs were shown; it was for ninety minutes with a lot of adult content. We both were involved in the movie; we enjoyed watching the movie. We saw the man with his wife and the other woman having multiple sexual encounters. It was exciting, interesting, sexually rejuvenating stuff.

Watching this movie would put a person on a high. Absolutely, it was not porn, which I would never allow him to see. I don't know, but he's not addicted to porn. It's really not recommended. The movie finished on a happy note. The wife lived with the husband, and the other lady went away on a job assignment to another country. Generally, maybe many aspects in that movie were true in real life; most movies are about true stories.

I got up, finished nature's call, went back, switched off the lights and the TV, and was ready to get into bed. My man, my stud of a man, was in his birthday suit; he was looking at me with the intention to have a good time. I was happy, and I slowly started undressing. He said, 'Wait.' He removed my top, my bra, my panties, and we both were as naked as new-born babies.

He started fondling me slowly, rubbing me, and he had a way to get me aroused. He was patient, but at the same time, he was in a hurry—not in a great hurry, but the intensity of that act to be consummated was always there. I think it's a trait of a man to be in an eternal hurry.

I told him, 'Sit down and let me take care of you.'

He said, 'No, today it is my turn. Yesterday night was your turn.'

He made me turn on my back, and I was positioned like a doggy. I was on all fours, and I knew what was coming. He adjusted me, and he entered my vagina. It was hot and full of vibrations. I had seen many of my female customers who had dildos, but I'd never allowed them to use them on me. When you can have a natural one, why use an artificial one?

So he went slowly into me, and I liked the way he did it; he did not to give me any discomfort. And he started stroking me in all directions. He moved his hips in three-sixty-degree motions, clockwise and anticlockwise. He moved in many different angles to make me feel happy, and slowly one of his fingers touched my clitoris. I was getting double the pleasure.

He slowly built me up. I was getting that hotness building up in me. My whole body was aching for more of it, and I wanted him to do it faster and quicker. He matched my movements. He understood my mood, and he kept on moving quickly and in a very controlled way. I could feel his organ was becoming bigger and bigger.

I had seen and felt that it was never the same length; it was different. But I was told by my guy, who was an expert in sex (as he called himself), that only the first two and a half inches matter when you enter the vagina to get a great orgasm. A longer penis is helpful in touching the G spot in many positions. A guy with a smaller penis has to adopt total-penetration postures, like the doggie and with the lady on top, to touch the G spot. Later on, it's only a sheath where the penis goes and touches the G spot in a female. There is a G spot that is deep inside the vagina, and when a man properly enters a woman, he can hit the G spot of the woman.

I think he was hitting my G spot. I was totally in a trance. I was totally enjoying it, and it was a great feeling. At that moment, I was hot.

I was telling him, 'Come on, finish it. Do it.'

And he said, 'Yes, me too, I'm ready.'

He kept on pumping, and there was a fullness of mind. He hit the peak, and it was bingo. We reached our climax, and it was a great shout of 'We did it!' It was a great volcanic eruption. We lost track of time. Again, I'm bringing in the philosophy that it is being one with the maker; it is being one with the god. It's a touch of godliness, being one with the creator. It's being one with your preserver. That's exactly what happens when you reach the pinnacle, the high. It is the ecstasy of pain and pleasure.

I enjoyed it. I would have had no problem if I'd died at that moment. We don't know where we go when we die; there are a lot of theories, but no one knows. No one knows if it's heaven or hell. He was totally happy, and he was very silent.

'What are you doing?'

'Nothing, I'm tired.'

'I understand.' I just slumped on to the bed. He was on top of me and still inside me. He was taking his weight on his hands. After some time, he slowly withdrew and went into the bathroom. We got into bed, and we held each other for a long time, looking at each other, holding each other. Then we slipped into a nice, deep sleep never to get up until the next morning.

Chapter 14

The morning of the third day was a good morning. We got ready by eight o'clock, rushed for our breakfast; we were famished. We had a little more than what we normally had—an extra glass of juice and an extra toast and then a bowl full of fruits. I had my usual ham, pork, rice, a bit of noodles, some chicken curry, and some pastries. After a nice cup of tea, we went back to our room. We relaxed up to ten o'clock. We had no program as such for the third day, so we ventured out to the hotel pool, started swimming for half an hour or so, and then we thought of going to the beach.

We had to climb down quite a few steps to go to the beach in front of our hotel. It was normally an open beach, where anybody could walk in, but a certain portion was being technically reserved for the use of guests of the hotel. There were many adjustable wooden beds and chairs set up with umbrellas to protect us from the sun. We ventured out into the sea, to where the water was up to our chests, but the guy who took care of the swimmers, the life guard, told us not to go further. We rode on the waves, and the waves pushed us back to the shore; it was fun and interesting. It was safe to venture into the sea if the green flag was hoisted to say that it was safe for us to swim. We had such a good time playing in the sand, swimming. We were shouting, laughing, and enjoying the swim.

We went back to the shore and lay down on one side of the wooden beds. Wearing our sunglasses, we tried to catch up with some sleep. There were many couples, single guys, all playing some kind of game. The sun was hot. The Europeans and the Americans wanted their skin to be tanned, and there were many who were applying lotions and lying down, changing positions to get that great tan. Maybe when they went back home, they would show their tans to their friends and feel proud, I supposed. I could see their skin turning from white to red.

It was one o'clock. We were there for almost two, three hours at the beach. We slowly went back and took a shower so that we wouldn't take more sand into the hotel premises. We went back to our room, took a shower again, and we ordered food in the room—some rice and some *tom yam pla*.

Pla is 'fish'. Tom yam is a nice spicy soup, one with plenty of ginger, chillies, and all the spices put in, plus basil leaves and many greens, mushrooms, and tomatoes; it's an excellent dish. I love it. Tom yam, I think, is the national dish. You can do it with any combination; it can be with pork, chicken, fish, prawns—anything.

We were not very hungry, but we were hungry, so we finished our food, then we slept. We both were tired after the swim in the pool and the beach. The food was filling, and then we went into a deep sleep.

We got up in the evening, around six, six thirty. I went into the bathroom to finish my needs. I came out with an apologetic smile and maybe a little bit concerned.

I was looking at my guy, and he asked, 'What? What happened?'

I said, 'I'm one week ahead of my normal period.'

He said, 'Okay, it's fine.'

Then I said, 'I don't have a sanitary pad.'

And he said, 'No problem.' Then he put on his shorts and T-shirt, rushed out, and came back in a short time. Then I just thanked him through my eyes. I went back into the bathroom, used the sanitary pad, and came out.

Then I was holding his hand and said, 'Sorry, I thought it is next week.'

He said, 'Fine, absolutely nothing to worry about. Anything can happen. It is fine.'

I said, 'I could have taken some tablet as a precaution to postpone.'

He said, 'No need. We had such a beautiful two days, and today is the third day. Absolutely no problem.'

This was what I liked about him; he was not disappointed—maybe a little as all humans react to a situation like this. I could say that he's a big-hearted man who understands my feelings and problems; that's where he scores.

He said, 'Come, let's go for a walk. Are you comfortable?'

I said, 'I'm fine. I have no problems in my three days. Thank the god mine is not a painful one. It's almost for two and a half days. That's my cycle, then it settles down.'

We dressed and went for a long walk on the beach. The sky was lit with a lot of stars, and the moon was almost full. A lot of light it was emitting; with the good air, the sound of waves, it was beautiful. At a distance, we could see many lights of maybe an island. It was scenic, beautiful, soothing, calm, and lovely. We walked for almost an hour, and slowly we returned the other way around through the roadside, looking at people. There were many youngsters and middle-aged and old people walking hand in hand, enjoying themselves.

That day we decided to go for Indian food. I, for one, did not like much of the oily stuff; well, it was good to try everything. We had some Indian bread; some chicken barbeque called chicken tikkas, spicy ones (they were good); some fish curry; and rice. Then we had sweets for my sweet-tooth man—a brown-to-deep-brown milk concentrate mixed with plain flour and a pinch of cardamom and salt, then rolled into small balls and nicely fried in oil. It is called *jamoon*; it's put in sugar syrup. It was too sweet, but it had a lot of cream. It was okay, and he relished it and had two portions. There was music on the background, some nice music, different. It was instrumental, and the melodies were nice to hear; we enjoyed it.

We paid the bill, tipped the bearer, and we went back to our room. We changed. I was all the time apologetic to him through my eyes. He gave me a look, reprimanding me, 'Don't be silly. Relax.' Then we hugged each other. I was on his chest, lying down, and I slowly slipped into a contented sleep. I didn't know, but he must have slowly moved me to my pillow. He tucked me in, and then he must have slept peacefully. Maybe he got his rest after two days of real sexual activity. So that was the third day.

On the fourth day, we got up, and I went to the bathroom first, took a nice shower, took care of myself, and went out with a big smile. He hugged me and kissed me on my cheeks and on my forehead. 'Sit, relax, dress. I'll go and get ready.' I was happy I could see his genuine smile. There was no discomfort on his face, and I was very happy with that kind of attitude. We got ready, went for our breakfast, went back, and then we started planning for the day.

'What should we do today?'

I said, 'Whatever you like.'

'Yes, today is a very calm and quiet day. It's a day when you should not be straining yourself, and you need a lot of rest.'

I said, 'Come on, I'm a sports person. I have no such problem. Let's go somewhere.'

He said, 'No.'

We went into the indoor game room of the hotel that had a carom board, ludo, snakes and ladders. You know, in the snakes-and-ladders game, you start from 1 and end in 100; that's where you finish. My man, who knows all the mysteries of the East, started saying that in India they have a game similar to snakes and ladders. There are a lot of ladders and a lot of snakes, and you have to roll a dice. Whatever the number that comes, you move accordingly. If a snake bites you, you go down, and if you find a ladder, you go up. When you complete the hundred steps starting from 1, you go to heaven. And if you are bitten by snakes all the time, you're down and struggling and will end up in hell. It all depends on if you're a nice guy, a good guy, then you go to heaven faster; if you're an evil man or evil woman or a sly guy, you'll be repeatedly bitten by the snakes.

I laughed out loud. He said, 'It is a similar thing to the snakes-and-ladders game. Okay, let's try it out.' So I took my usual blue colour, and my guy took the yellow. So we started rolling the dice, and it went on. We both were continuously getting the ladder; at the same time, we were also getting bitten by snakes. Finally, maybe after half an hour, we both almost reached the hundredth point, and I suppose, we were welcomed into heaven.

Then we played a game of carom. So it was ladies first. It's always the white pawn for the guy, who strikes first, and the game ends with twenty-nine points. Red is five, the white is two, and the black is one. So we were both good at it, and it was neck to neck, and finally, I won the game. He applauded me. He came up from the opposite seat, where he was sitting, and he gave me a good kiss. He said, 'Well done.' I was very happy. He appreciated my win, and he wasn't bothered by his loss. Maybe he was trying to please me, but I could see he was genuine; it was a good gesture from him.

Then we had a game of chess. I was not very efficient; I did not have much knowledge of it. He taught me the game; he made me understand the pawns, the rooks, the horses, the bishops, the minister, the king, and the queen. The minister is very powerful, but if the king is checkmated, the whole game will collapse. I understood half. I said, 'Fine. I'll learn.' I played. I knew I could not win, but I did try my best. I picked up the best of three. Maybe he made me win the game to make me happy. It became two on two (my one win in carom and one in chess and his two in chess), so we both were even—women's liberation, fifty–fifty equality in life, and progress.

It was almost one thirty. We went to a shop opposite the hotel. We took some burgers. He had a vegetable burger, and I took a chicken burger. It was a big-sized one, but so be it, and I wanted a Cola. Again, the lectures started. Although the lectures he would give had meaning, he had already lectured me on many things. Maybe it was because he was more experienced because of his age; he had seen the world.

He said, 'Any soft drink with a lot of fizz in it—whether it's a cola, an orange, or even a watery, coloured stuff—is not good for the health. The bubbles in the soda takes three days for them to be digested in our system, so it's much safer to drink fresh fruit juice or coffee or tea.'

I said, 'Fine. I give up.'

I took an orange juice, freshly made, and he went for a nice cup of tea. So that became our brunch instead of lunch—no rice.

He said, 'We'll have a beautiful dinner with a lot of rice.'

I said, 'Fine.'

We went back to the room because it was hot outside. Just crossing the road itself, we were sweating. We went in, took a shower (the second one in the day), and we both slept. I fell asleep instantly maybe due to my period. He was watching a silent movie. The TV was on, and he didn't want to disturb my sleep, so there was no volume. Eventually, he must have also slept for a little while.

I got up at five, six o'clock. I took another shower, got ready, and went for a walk—again, a long walk. We became familiar with the main street of Krabi. We didn't venture into any of the side streets at night-time; maybe it was safe but not very advisable.

That day we went back to the Thai restaurant. We had prawns, red curry, rice, chicken satay, some stir-fried fish, and more rice. Live Thai music was on, and beautiful songs were being sung by a man and a lady. It was so serene, so quiet. We had some beer for a change. My guy didn't like to drink beer because he had a bit of a gout problem. Once in a while, he liked it. It was fine; a glass of beer wouldn't harm. So the food was divine, and so was the music. Music changes your mood; it brings you to a higher level of relaxation. You understand the mundane life and its intricacies. We were there for almost two hours, listening to the songs.

That day surprisingly my man said, 'No sweets.'

I laughed out loud. 'What? You don't want that extra power today?'

'Because you have no action,' he said. 'Not like that. Too much of sweets is not good for the health.'

'Okay. I accept. Fine.' We Thais don't like to eat sweets.

We slowly, lazily walked back to our room, settled down, and we decided we would catch up with our sleep instead of watching TV. He said he would like to watch some news. I said, 'Fine.' I turned to the other side and slept again. Without any sound, he was taking in the news, and I was sure he must have also slept after some time, so that was that. The fourth day passed quietly, and we had one more day left before going back.

The fifth day was our final day in Krabi, and we wanted to make it a more memorable one. We got up early as we had plenty of rest, had breakfast, and we were ready by nine o'clock. So we got into a tuk-tuk, a three-wheeler auto rickshaw; it makes a lot of noise, but it is very convenient to use in narrow streets and roads. Normally the driver is an expert guy; he can go into any small lanes, by-lanes. We engaged a guy who was very talkative and eager to make us happy. He said he would take us to all the nice places and that we should keep our cameras ready. We worked out the fare for half a day. The price was fixed.

He took us to a flower show. There were many beautiful flowers of different colours. We had not seen many such varieties. It was real fun taking photographs, and from there, we went to a museum, where they had kept many artefacts of many centuries old. There were many Buddha statues; some were antique ones, maybe hundreds of years old, all nicely preserved. There were nameplates of Buddha depicting his different stages of prayers and his different names. Some statues showed him in deep meditation or in deep penance for the good of others. Monks in olden days ate very little for days and months, sometimes nothing at all, not even water at times. Those were the days of that kind of people with great calibre, capacity, concentration, and will to achieve being one with the god.

We started to climb a small mountain. There was a beautiful Buddha temple there. The lord sitting in meditation was so calming and soothing to our souls. We worshiped, and there was a monk who blessed us. We put in some money into the box; we took the blessings to make us happy and to make everybody else also happy. I think charity begins at home, and we want the whole universe to be happy. It's a very lofty thought, but in this busy world, no one has time to even think of it. Apart from this kind of thought, we walked up to a small point, and from there we could see the whole town. It was nice and beautiful.

We enjoyed the view, took photographs, and the driver brought us back almost to the main street of Krabi.

Then the man said, 'What do you want for lunch?'

We said, 'Yes, we'd like to have a good meal.'

'I'll take you to a very nice place. You'll get beautiful food.'

We said we were game. He took us to a small shack. The man and the lady of the small hotel welcomed us. They made us comfortable. They gave us some coconut water squeezed with lime, which is a great elixir for the body. They took twenty minutes to serve hot rice, tom yam with plenty of small prawns thrown in, fish nicely cooked in charcoal, and some barbeque stuff. It was a great fare with a lot of spices—spicy but unique and out of this world. We enjoyed it; we invited the driver also to join us. All three of us shared the meal. The guy was happy, and we were very happy with the food.

Surprisingly, the cost of the food was half of what we normally paid in one of those fancy restaurants on the main street. We had such good food, and it was wonderful— pomfret fish that was big-size, snow white (the colour of the flesh once you remove the skin), well cooked, spicy, and piping hot. When you have a good meal and you're satisfied, you whole body is at peace, and you feel contented. You feel that there's nothing else left in life. For one minute, if you are just quiet, I think that is one with divinity. After that meal, they offered us some more coconut water. It was so sweet, and we couldn't eat the flesh of the coconut; we were totally full.

The tuk-tuk man, the auto man, asked us, 'How was your meal, sir?'

We said, 'Great, sir.'

We were mighty pleased. He drove us back to the hotel, and we paid him his money.

He said, 'Anywhere else you want to go? Call me.' He gave me his number.

We said, 'Sir, tomorrow we go back to the airport, back to Bangkok.'

He said, 'I wish you'd be here for another day. I would've taken you to another village where you could have eaten such fantastic food.'

We said, 'Maybe next time. Thank you.'

We parted with the guy and went back to our room. We were totally full, and then we sat down on the sofa and turned on the TV to the news channel.

'Any news channel in any given day shows some calamity somewhere in the world, some accidents, some thefts, some political problems. There is no such news as social activity and help carried out to solve public grouses. It's always chaos, problems. People like to watch problems and chaos, and I think everybody gets a vicarious pleasure in the suffering of other humans. I don't know. That's what I feel.'

My wise man said, 'It is not like that. This is how the world is made. Everybody wants all the good, the best, and the pleasures, but it's one side of the coin. The whole world is made of duality. When there is good, there is bad. When there's day, there's night. And if there is light, there is darkness. You can keep on comparing. So it's a cycle. You have to go through the process. Then only you will come out of your karma, your fate, your destiny. It's not always a bed of roses. Even a rose bush has a lot of thorns, and you will have to slowly pluck the beautiful rose flower. It is said that we should accept life as it comes and go along with the tide. If today is bad, tomorrow may be good. If tomorrow is good, the day after may be bad. But not necessarily—maybe a couple of good days and a couple of bad days. That's how life goes on.'

Then he coyly looked at me and said, 'Look, we had two great days of sex and now two great days of no sex. That's how it is. Today is the fifth day. How are you feeling?'

I told him, 'I don't know. Maybe tonight if I'm okay.'

He said, 'No problem.'

'I know what you mean. I can understand your eagerness,' I said. 'Let's see what happens tonight. It's a mystery, as you say. Your divinity will decide what's going to happen.'

He said, 'Totally up to our karma. If we are destined, we will have that kind of pleasure. Yes, it will definitely happen.'

I said, 'Okay, let's see now what are we going to do.'

'Yes. We are full,' he said. 'Normally, I don't sleep in the afternoon when I'm busy on my job, but now it's a holiday. Let's sleep when you can sleep. It's good to sleep eight hours a day, but normally, six or seven hours is fine.'

I told him, 'I sometimes sleep only for two to three hours if I am very busy with my customers when I'm on total work.'

He said, 'I understand. Don't worry. Things will change. It's a cycle, and in your life, all the thorns will be slowly removed. You will blossom into a beautiful flower that's useful to many people with your great fragrance.'

I told him, 'Don't become a poet. You now go to sleep.'

That was how our afternoon ended with sleep. In the evening, we visited a program going on in the concert hall (called the town hall). It was an entertainment program organized by the youths of Krabi. We bought our tickets; the hotel guys helped us with the tickets, which were two hundred baht per person. We had our front-row seats. It was a program of three hours. A lot of jokers and a lot of actors, actresses, and musicians—it was a big crowd. There might have been one thousand five hundred people. So the show started. There were plenty of jokes and beautiful stories from *Ramayana*, an epic from India.

You know, Thailand's culture is built on many influences. There is a bit from Brahmanism of India. There's a bit of Zen from China, and we have our own folk culture from the Siam region. This mixture of Asian cultures forms the basis of our Thai culture. Now we have the new culture added from the Americans.

So the show was a mixture of old music, modern music, rock music, and all kinds of rap music. There were tales from the olden days and many Indian-, Chinese-, and Thai-themed stories presented with girls nicely dressed for that period, dances, music, and dialogues. It was totally awe-inspiring. We were all totally involved, and the locals were glued to the stage. It was a great live performance. My guy, though, did not understand the language, but seeing is believing. He was carried away by the program, and he was totally enjoying it. It was so vibrant. There were so many young people. Their bodies were so flexible, and they could do so many acrobatic things. We looked at their creation, at the program offered by these people who were really very ordinary folks. They were dedicated and so involved in maintaining the culture of Thailand.

After three hours of the program, it ended with all the actors, actresses, jokers, musicians going to the stage. They bowed down to us, and a tremendous amount of clapping and appreciation was shown. There was the usual practice of a tip box being placed at the exit. All the actors and actresses mingled with the crowd at the first and second row. The unruly crowd who were on the balcony and behind tried to reach out to them.

So we tipped them and shook hands with many. A lot of Europeans, Americans, Asians, Japanese, and Vietnamese were there, a big mixed crowd of tourists. We had such a beautiful time. After the program, we thought it was safe to eat Thai food because the next day we were going to fly back to Bangkok.

'Known devil is better than the unknown.'

'It's not a devil. It's an angel.'

'Known angel is better than the unknown.'

So we had our usual fare. It was always fish for my man. That day we had some pork for a change and some prawn rice. We filled ourselves with food at a mediocre joint where the food was excellent as per the recommendation of our hotel man. He was right. The food was extremely good. The price was reasonable, not very expensive. So we saved some money.

Slowly walked back to our hotel, and we were tired after three hours of concentrating on the program on the stage and the food we had tucked in. I went into the bathroom, went back, and he was looking at me.

I said, 'Fifty—fifty.'

He said, 'What?'

'Maybe or maybe not. There is a very small trickle. I think we can manage safely—not on the bed,' I said. 'Well, maybe in the bathtub.'

He said, 'I am game. Let us have some rest.'

We sat on the sofa. It was only nine o'clock. We had one more CD ready from the receptionist, a nice English movie with adult content. I think it was an old movie with Marilyn Monroe, and I don't remember the name of the guy. She was a gorgeous woman—just beautiful, sexy. We heard a lot of interesting tales of big guys, influential top guys in political circles, being with her. The movie was interesting, sexy, and Marilyn symbolized eternal flow of youth and its exploitation. We are not the judges of others as we are to be judged by our own conscience.

We finished the movie, and it was ten thirty or so. So I went for my inspection. I came out with a big smile and said, 'We can but still not on the bed. The sheets may become dirty.'

He said, 'Yes, let's not trouble the hotel people.'

So we went into the bathroom and got into the bathtub. He just lay down on his back. I slowly started kissing him from his chest onwards, and he was up, ready. His penis was totally looking at my vagina; it was stiff and erect. I slowly removed my sanitary pad, washed once again, and slowly let him enter me. He was totally excited. It had been two days, and he was hungry for me. The holiday mood, the good food, and the rest had rejuvenated him. I was also eager, so we both locked ourselves. I started moving, he started moving, and believe me, in a matter of two minutes, we both achieved our orgasms. He poured into me, and I was also pouring my cum into him. It was a beautiful finish, and we were like that for five, ten minutes.

He started losing his erection. He wanted to pull out. I was on top, and I allowed him out. There were a few residues of blood on his penis. I slowly washed them out and soaped him. He soaped me, and we took a shower together, cleaned ourselves, kissed, hugged, got out of the bathtub, and dried ourselves. We were satiated; we were happy. It was a quick one but a nice one from two days of abstinence. We both walked back to the bed, hugged, kissed, and we slept, our two bodies as one, covering ourselves. I think the sleep god embraced us, and it was a beautiful ending to our fifth day.

The day of completion of our holiday was the sixth day, a lucky number for me and to him. Yes, I was born on the sixth. If you believe in numerology, six denotes success and money. I could make big money. I was pleased to hear this from my guy, and that was the start of our day. We had a good breakfast. We slowly went back to our room, started packing, and went out for a walk in the hot sun just to get the feel and to say bye to the town of Krabi. We purchased a few things which I wanted. Then by eleven, eleven thirty, we were in our room, and we had another one hour to go to the airport.

We thought it was time to do something with ourselves. He was holding me. I was also wrapped around him. We were feeling nice, and we just wanted to be like that for a minute. I thought time should stop. We should be like that. Yes, mentally, we could be, not physically. Our bodies had varied activities. We were just holding each other, and he was telling me he would go back today from heaven to earth to his environment to face life as it unfolded. I would go back to my working station in Pattaya and my activities in attending to my customers, doing massages, making a living, and taking care of my family. I said yes and then I asked him when he would come back. He said, 'Definitely within a period of three months.' We discussed the rough dates to match my menstrual cycle. It was very difficult to pinpoint because it varied.

If I had no sexual activity, the periods were more are less stable, but it was unstable when I did have sex, though I usually didn't have sex without him. There might be some exceptional customers with good money, and sex with them was without my total involvement. Of course, my body would react, and I'd get an orgasm. I wouldn't say no, but it was not coming from my heart; it was happening to my body. See, there is a difference in how the body reacts whether it is with A or B or X or Y or Z, but if it's with someone whom you really love, whom you really care about, whom you really want, the end result is much nicer; it is very touching and makes you more fulfilled.

He understood my feelings. He said, 'I do know how things happen.' He was pleading his inability to take care of me fully and to be with me because of his earlier commitments and having his own duties. He was a man of certain convictions, certain duties. We Easterners are very emotional, we get attached, we stick to our commitments for as long as possible, and we try to see that we carry out our promises and fulfil our commitments without fail.

We were just together. He was looking into my eyes. He was getting excited. The parting, the going away must have stirred him or stirred his greed to have me one more time. It was the same act, it was the same movements, but each time, it was a different activity, a different touch, different emotions, and different results. People say two fingers are not the same, and I understood his need.

I slowly undressed. I made him take off his clothes, and we were eager. He started kissing me, tonguing me, and he was sucking my nipples and breasts out of greed. I was getting excited; I was slowly feeling the hotness spreading all over my body. He went down. He tongued my clit, and he was inside my vagina. Then he kissed my thighs; all over my body, he was kissing me. I was ready. We got into the missionary position; he entered me up to the hilt. It was strong, healthy, big; the whole of his organ was inside me. The depth of the vagina and the length of the penis can never be properly measured; these depend on the situation and the circumstances.

He started moving. I started moving. We were building up, and he wanted to change our position. He made me stand, and I was against the wall, one leg on his hips. He entered my vagina, and he lifted me up. Both my legs were locked on his back, and he started moving. It was a total penetration. He started moving. I was seeing heaven, and it was beautiful. He was panting and was totally ready. Then he again put me on the bed, and it was a furious pumping. I also matched his stride, and it was one big go and a big come. It was a great feeling; we had not taken more than ten, fifteen minutes. We had thought we would never have sex that morning, but you know, it finally led to that.

The human mind is always greedy. At that parting shot of intimacy, our happiness was overwhelming. He slowly withdrew. We took a shower together, fondling, kissing, holding, and slowly dressed. The phone rang. Reception said our car for the airport was ready, and we said, 'Give us five to ten minutes.' We dressed. We were totally packed, and we called for the bellboy. Our luggage was taken. We said bye to the receptionist, tipped the guy and the housekeeping people; they were the ones who took care of room cleaning. We always tipped the housekeeping people.

It was a half-hour, forty-minute ride to the airport. It was my second flight. We waited for the flight to come in, then got into the aircraft. It was the same chatty crowd full of foreigners all excited. The flight took off, and after one hour or so, we landed at Suvarnabhumi Airport. We picked up our luggage and went out. He had a lot of time, and I volunteered to stay with him.

He said, 'No, you're tired. Go back. You have to go back another 120 kilometres back to Pattaya. You go relax, sleep, and get ready for your work tomorrow.'

I shook my head. He said, 'Why not talk?'

I was emotional. It was a great six days with him. I was feeling like I was a part of him. He was my man, my soulmate, my friend, my guide, my philosopher. I was sure he also felt the same.

We were together in the coffee shop for maybe half an hour, one hour. He went down to the ground level, and I bought my ticket for the bus to Pattaya City. He waited and saw me get into the bus. I waved at him. He waved and he said 'Bye, see you next time' through sign language. My bus left. He was emotional. His eyes were misty. I understood that the feeling was mutual.

And that was how I returned back to my job. The next day, he called me from his place. He was home and back to his job. I said I was in my surroundings and was waiting for him to come.

Chapter 15

After the trip to Krabi, I was so refreshed. It was a new experience, and life had more of a pep in it. I was in touch with my guy, and we were talking once in a week, maybe once in two weeks. Time rolled, and three months passed, then I got a call from him saying that he was coming. I was overjoyed. As usual, the excitement, the inner feelings stirred, and I was waiting for him to come.

Meanwhile, I called my people and told them that he was coming. Then they said, 'Why don't you bring him home? We have a big event where our revered monk who passed away three years ago is celebrated on his anniversary day. There will be a big celebration, and big ceremonies will take place in honour of him.'

In our village, the body of our revered monk was preserved in the wat—that is, the temple. He was a very noble, wise, and elevated guy in his meditations and teachings. His body had been put in a casket and was kept on a pedestal near the foot of the Buddha statue inside the temple. Once a year, there was a time for big celebrations for this monk. The body was shifted from the temple and put on a high pedestal for devotees' viewing. We all would go to him, prostate, look at the body, and walk beneath the body to get the grace from him.

My dad, my mom, my friends said, 'Bring him and let him enjoy the festivity of Thailand.'

I said, 'I will try. I'll ask him.'

The minute I saw him coming, my heart raced fast and furious. We both were excited. He had called me from the airport earlier, and he came around ten o'clock. I was ready and waiting for him. He saw me, and he was all smiles. He held my hand, and we checked into the hotel room. We both were eager to be together after a long gap of time. We hugged each other. He was in his elements, and we had a quick mating session. He was all over me. I was all over him. We did what we were missing in the last three months. We repeated many of the things we had done in Krabi, which freshened up our memories. We were all so built up. It was a matter of four, five minutes, and we both were spent. He had a big one, and I had a big orgasm. Then we both were floating and seeing the god, the one who could give us so much of happiness and pleasure.

We both lay down on the bed, and I slowly asked him, 'How are you, and how is your work?' I tried to know more about him.

He was surprised and said, 'You're very happy to see me, and I think you have a program on your mind. After Krabi, what is your plan?'

I said, 'How can you guess my thoughts? Are you a mentalist or what?'

'I know how women are. If they want anything to be done, normally it's before sex, but they ask favours after sex, when a man is very happy and in a receptive mood, willing to listen, accept, and offer whatever favour is asked.'

I told him, 'There is going to be a big festivity in our village temple, where our revered monk, who passed away three years ago, will be celebrated on his third death anniversary. We have preserved his body, and in his honour, we'll be having a nice three-day function. Why not we go there?'

He said, 'Okay, I'm ready. What about the booking here?'

I said, 'It is not an issue. I will talk to the reception.' I knew everybody in the hotel where the massage shop was located; it was part of the hotel set-up. We ate some breakfast, and I told him to sleep and relax. He had a long flight and must be tired with no sleep overnight.

'You sleep and let me organize the program, and then we can go.'

He said, 'As you wish.'

Then I rushed out. I took a two-wheeler from my friend and then went out and planned the trip through my travel agent. Then I told them to arrange the train ticket to go to Sisaket. My guy preferred to go in a train, not in a bus. He felt it was not very comfortable. We did have very nice buses, but still, a bus journey was a bus journey. I finished all my pending work at the massage shop.

At lunchtime, I went to his room, and he was still sleeping. I woke him up. I had bought some nice papaya—you know, the spicy one—and a lot of tomatoes and vegetables, a bit of crab and raw mango, raw papaya and rice noodles all mixed together with a lot of chillies in it. It was a very spicy fare. Along with that, I had a lot of fresh green spinach, which contains a lot of nutrients. With the papaya, we had some of the food he had brought along, and our stomachs were full. After a bit of rest, he suggested we go for a swim. We swam for quite some time, and it was very relaxing.

I told him, 'Tomorrow morning, we check out, go to Bangkok, and catch a train to Sisaket.'

He said, 'Fine. I'm all yours. Plan it as you wish.'

I had managed to give my massage work to other girls. They were too eager to accept it because they would earn more money. So I went out with him. We took a long walk on the beach and had some tender coconuts. You know, in Thailand we have such beautiful, most-healthy, tender coconuts. One coconut can fill your stomach. Sometimes there is one litre of water inside, and of course, the flesh of the coconut is very sweet.

So we had coconut, walked, squatted to enjoy the view and fresh air. Many lovers were walking around. Many girls were looking for lovers. Many old men were limping around to gain more strength to their tired legs. There were plenty of people—all kinds, all colours, big, fat, medium, thin, lean, good-looking, handsome, mediocre, not handsome—but everybody had one thing in common. They were all smiling, they were all excited, and they were all in anticipation of pleasures.

Look at the happiness. Look at the pleasures. A person can get almost anything in Pattaya. They will forget all their problems. They may not be walking regularly in their countries since they're very busy making money, but here they walk, eat good and different healthy food, and meet a lot of new people; there's the attraction of getting a beautiful female. They may have a lot of restrictions, taboos, commitments in their place of residence from all over the world, whereas in Pattaya it's heaven on earth. If you just wish to have a girl, yes, it's fulfilled just like that—no hazards, no cop problems. Nowhere else it is possible.

We finished our walk and went back to the room. I told him to give me two, three hours and I would join him for the night. Of course, on the way back to the room, we had our dinner in our usual place. We were welcomed by our friends in the eating joint—a big hall where there were many small, small shops. They can make a fresh-fish dish with chillies and lemon sauce, or a sizzler—anything we wanted to eat. Prawns, fish, meat, eggs, chicken, pork—everything was available in plenty. We had good fish and rice, and then we went back to the room.

I said, 'I'll finish my pending work and come back.'

He said, 'Okay.'

He enjoyed watching TV; he liked all the Thai soaps, where we had a lot of good girls, bad girls, and beautiful girls all fighting and trying to find the best man for themselves. Normally, there would be a triangle going on in Thai soaps on TV. I had two customers, and I finished my part of the massage work.

Then I told the cashier, 'My guy has come. Can I go to him?'

She said, 'Go.' She shifted my number back, and other girls took over.

I rushed back to him and knocked on the door. He was eagerly waiting for me. Then we were together, hugging each other for a few minutes, and then we settled down for the night.

I went for my wash, changed. I had carried a small bag with my essential needs, which I used whenever he visited me. I got into my nightdress, and he held me and started kissing me and hugged me for some time.

Then I said, 'What is the hurry?'

He said, 'I was missing you all these three months after the trip to Krabi. I just wanted to feel you.'

I said, 'Feel me. No problem.'

Then he smiled at me, and he was laughing. We both settled down. We were holding our hands, and we started chatting.

He asked me, 'How was our trip to Krabi?'

I said, 'It was divine. I always think of it. It was beautiful.'

I thought he was going to be in Pattaya for ten days; that was normally his program. This time, he had twelve days. That was what he said.

I said, 'Fine. No problem. We're already minus one night. Tomorrow morning, we'll be leaving for Bangkok, then onwards to Sisaket by train.'

He was happy to make me happy. I told him about the big event which would take place in the temple.

He heard me, and he told me, 'See how civilization or society which has evolved has presented many aspects of life. The feeling of good, the feeling of bad—those come from within you. When you do something which you think is right, again it's the inculcation from your childhood, the pattern set into your system by your surroundings, by your people. You take that as the role model, and you think that is the best. And it's reinforced by many such incidents until you're seven years old. Seven is a very important number. Every seven years, a person's life changes as per astrology.'

I listened to him. He was a wise man. I took his talks seriously.

He further said, 'After seven years, your mind is set on a certain pattern. For anything else anybody says other than what you believe in, you will take it always with a pinch of salt. There is a possibility of you changing your thought processes if you feel whatever the other guy says is right. That is the reason you get attached to certain things in life. Let's say it's a doll, and you dress it up, you talk to it, you keep it with you, you hug it, and it's soft and nice. And then you get so attached to it. You can't leave it for even a minute, even when you go to your school. But at some stage, when you find something else which gives you more joy, which gives you more happiness, and which makes you more excited, you'll give up the doll. You'll feel that the newfound joy is more attractive than the doll. Let's say it's riding a bicycle or riding a motorized bike which gives you more happiness and is more exciting. So this is technically compared to the meanings of life. When you find a higher or bigger joy, you drop the lower or smaller joy. This is how life evolves, and it is a multiple joy. First, your doll and then your bicycle, and when you become an adult, you will want the proximity of a woman or a man. The feminine voice attracts the man, the manly figure attracts the woman, and they love to chat and spend time together. They steal a kiss, they hug, they touch, and all of this is so exciting. They feel that is the only thing in the world, that nothing else is required. They are not bothered by anything else. So it goes on from one to another. Then comes a guy who wants to make more money. So he falls into the trap of moneymaking.'

I asked my guy, 'Am I after money?'

'Yes, you are, but a stage will come when you will say, "Enough of money. I need more peace and happiness."'

I said, 'No, I need money.'

'Done. Fine. Right now, yes, you need money,' he said. 'Then don't interrupt. Listen to my explanation.'

I said, 'Okay, fine, go ahead.'

Then he said, 'You're in a money trap. You're in a competition. You want to excel in the field of work you have chosen. You want to make a name for yourself. You want to become famous and rich. Everybody has a wish, and everybody wants to ride the dream horse. The horse has to be tamed like in the Old West. Yeah, the horse, which is virile, is full of spunk, the cowboy has to ride it and manage to tame it. I think it is called rodeo. Everybody wants a challenge. Everyone wants to prove to himself that he has the capacity and the power to achieve what generally is thought not achievable. Humans have that kind of feeling or that kind of enterprise. Today in life, everybody wants to achieve and excel. It's more materialistic, but it was not so in the olden days. In those days, people were very happy to succeed in their chosen field of work, either as an artist, sculptor, a soldier, or any other profession a person has chosen. So that's how life is.'

I told him, 'Fine. What are you trying to tell me?'

'I'm trying to tell you that your monk spent all his life practising austerity and died at the age of eighty five. His body is kept in a box with glass on all four sides. He's preserved, a holy man. We say "Ashes to ashes", but how is the body well preserved? There's no smell of it rotting. And how is it possible? Maybe they had put a lot of rare herbs. A beautiful silk sheet was put over him, and he's lying there majestically with his Buddha in him,' he said. 'This is how life unfolds. What you sow, you reap. The monk had sowed good seeds, helping people and making people understand the transient nature of life, the temporary feelings to control. Giving up the pleasures in life, denying himself, and finding that serenity—all these were being practised by the monk.'

I told him, 'Next year, after the fourth year, we'll be cremating him. That was his wish, and we're going to carry it out.'

My guy said, 'This is where you have to give a connection of how he led his life and why the society of the olden days was more peaceful. In the present day, everything is measured in terms of money, and everybody is told to make more money, to be happy, to buy all the physical pleasures.'

I told him, 'Come on.'

He said, 'Yes, that's it for the day.' Then we both sat after the religious sermon and watched TV for some time. There was a movie on one of the channels, and we started watching it.

Chapter 16

The movie had the same old theme—boy, girl, and villains revolving around their problems; love scenes; a bit of fighting; jealousy. Normally, today we have many female villains in Thai stories. But finally, the truth wins, and lovers are united to be happy forever. The whole audience are happy and emotionally touched. That's how the whole thing works. Everybody wants a happy ending. That included me and my soulmate.

After the movie, we both looked at each other.

I asked him, 'Are you tired? Do you want to sleep?'

He said, 'Yes, I want to sleep only after having some fun with you.'

I was surprised to see him in that kind of determined mood on his first day of visit. Maybe he had conserved his energy and his semen to share it with me. I haven't, believe me, so far asked him how he managed to be so focused on his sex life.

He had told me, 'It's a big, long story. Some time I will explain it to you. Already you think that whatever I say is a great philosophy, but it is not a philosophy. Philosophy stems from the true facts of life. People keep on presenting facts in such a way that the subject becomes dry and nobody is interested in it. But if it is spiced up and it's got a touch of sex, my god, the whole thing is full of energy because we're all made out of sexual energy. *Sex* is such a beautiful word.

Everybody lives for it from the smallest of species to the biggest.'

I said, 'Now it is one midnight. We have to get up early tomorrow for our journey to my home.' I told him to just lie down. 'You had your go in the morning. Now it's my time.'

He smiled at me. He undressed and later lay down. I took charge. I started kissing him all over. I slowly nibbled his chest; he didn't have breasts, but he had nipples. I just slowly tongued them. A man would get excited if you nibbled it or tongued it. And slowly, I went down, took his manhood, and slowly played with it; I slowly started sucking him and tickling his two balls. It must have tickled him, and he was getting excited. I told him to enjoy, that I won't take much time. I slowly started tonguing him, and he was getting excited. I lay down on him and started moving on him. It was more of a breast massage.

We both were naked, and I was on him, rotating on him, gyrating on him, feeling him. And I was using a bit of my hand to pleasure his back, his shoulders, then his thighs and legs. They were sort of slow, synchronized movements and changing spots, which could give a different feeling. He was relaxing, and he was enjoying it. I was there on him for almost ten minutes. He was totally relaxed. As he was totally relaxed, even his organ relaxed. I allowed him to relax for more time.

Again, I started building him up. I was kissing him. I was on top of him, and I slowly felt his manhood stirring. I took it in my hand, and I slowly introduced that into my vagina. Once it was in its home, it started growing. It always grew with the proper heat and the movement with the vagina. He started slowly moving.

I told him, 'Don't. Let me do it for you.' I again went down on him with his penis still inside me but slightly out.

As I told you guys earlier, you only need two-and-a-half inches to make a woman get excited. That's where the sensitive zones are located, which produce maximum pleasure for the woman. The balance of six, seven inches is all in the sheath.

So I was holding his hand. We were hand to hand, mouth to mouth; he was inside me, and I was moving. It was more like an exercise, like I was doing dips on both my hands. I went down and came up. I went down and came up with a small erotic sound; I was doing it. I had now grown stronger by doing many of these kinds of exercises on many of the bodies of my customers. Here I was on top of my guy, my soulmate, whom I loved, and I was on him without a condom. I could feel his fullness and flesh rubbing me, and it was a great pleasure.

You always enjoy whatever you do if you're doing that with the person you love and appreciate it. The happiness is immense. If the same thing is done only for the sake of doing it, it's just a mechanical affair. That is the reason most sex sessions done for money are not so tasteful, not so good. In the heat of things, you feel you had a great time, but if you really analyse it and think, you'll understand the true love, happiness, and pleasure which emanate from two people who really like or love each other. That's why there are still great stories of really great lovers, like Romeo and Juliet and so many other couples.

I was getting excited; he was building up. I could feel his erection was more than the usual. I shifted, and his penis was pulled out. It was all big, strong, and nice. I took it in my mouth for maybe five minutes. It was all big, nice, juicy, and wet. There was pre-cum inside me and on his penis. I felt he might come at any time. I put that back into my vagina, and I started moving. We started moving, and it was a big moment, like the whole world going into an explosion. And there came the big explosion of my cum and his semen all mixing together, a concoction of great feeling.

Every time I have this, I feel I'm seeing my Buddha. Maybe we're all trained to think of the god too much. Whichever religion we follow, always there is a link, a comparison, because it has been inculcated from our childhood. We tend to bring in a comparison—one with Buddha, one with my god, one with my creator, one with the universe, and one with godliness; that's how it is.

I was happy, and he was so pleased.

He said, 'My day is done. My life is blessed. I'm thankful to the power. Made me so happy.'

I told him, 'Okay, now you're a good boy. Go wash and come back.'

He said, 'You go. Let me relax. I know you're tired, but you can do it.'

I went and took a quick shower and came out. He went in, and we both were together. We got into the bed, hugged each other, and fell asleep.

In the morning, I was told that our train was departing at 8.30 p.m. in the night from the Bangkok Fort Station. There was a train in the morning, but it did not have an air-conditioned coach. The travel agent had organized two tickets for the eight thirty train in the night. It was okay with us. I woke him up, told him we had plenty of time and didn't need to rush. We both went down for breakfast in the hotel. He paid one hundred fifty baht for my breakfast.

Then after the good food, I told him, 'I'll go back, change, come back with my luggage, and we'll check out in the afternoon and catch a taxi to Bangkok by two, three o'clock.'

Then he said, 'Fine.'

We started our journey around three o'clock. We reached Bangkok, and the evening traffic was very heavy when we reached closer to Bangkok; it's a big city. We reached the Fort Station well ahead of time. We waited in the waiting hall, and the train came on to the track at eight o'clock. We found our coach. It was an air-conditioned coach with two beds—one on the lower level and the other one on the upper level. It was a little tiny for my tall man, but it was manageable. All the other Europeans and Americans travelling in these trains also found the beds not big enough for the tall men's standards. We were taught to adjust to the circumstances. 'Be a Roman in Rome' was what my guy said; I agreed with him.

It was hot outside. We got into the train. The air conditioner was on, and that made us comfortable. We took some water and soft drinks and green tea with flower extracts added and served ice cold. We had finished our dinner on the way to the station, and we settled down for the night.

The guy who took care of travelling comforts, the attendant, made our bed, put clean sheets on the mattress on top of the seat, and provided nice pillows and small blankets to cover ourselves with; they were clean and ironed ones. The travelling-ticket examiner checked our tickets, and we said goodnight.

He climbed up to the upper berth, and I was on the lower berth. We were to get up at seven o'clock in the morning to alight at Sisaket station.

He came down within fifteen minutes, and I asked him, 'What?'

He said, 'I'm going to the restroom.'

I said, 'Go and come back.'

He came back, then he sat down with me, and I said, 'Let's sleep.'

He said, 'You sleep, and I'll watch through the window.'

The outskirts of Bangkok were visible, the train was slowly moving. It would stop in many stations on the way to pick up more passengers. The train would go beyond Sisaket to Ubon. That was the last point, and then it would come back via Sisaket to Bangkok.

In Issan, the north-east of Thailand, all females are beautiful by the blessings of Buddha. See how proud we are. Though I have said many times beauty is skin-deep, beauty counts, and the colour counts. Everybody likes bright and beautiful things in life. Even the sheets put on the bed are white sheets. So they are the children of the higher god, the white ones, I suppose.

He was watching something, and I told him, 'I'm going to sleep.'

He said, 'Please sleep. I don't want anything.' Then he kissed me a few times, hugged me, touched me.

I told him, 'Don't get excited, not in the train. Go and be a good boy and sleep.'

The partitions in the train were very thin. Only we both were there in the first class coupe. We could lock our area from inside, and we could have privacy. There were around fifty people in the second class sleeper which is attached next to our coach. It had air conditioner, and it cost less money.

Then I told him, 'Go to sleep. Tomorrow we'll be home. You can have all the things you want to have.'

He smiled and said, 'Thank you.' He went up and slept.

We had a good sleep in spite of the train stopping in many stations. I had kept an alarm on my cell phone for around six o'clock in the morning. I woke him up, and at the same time, the attendant came and knocked on our doors, saying, 'Madam, Sisaket after three stops.' I told him, 'Thank you.' We got up and freshened ourselves. We got out of the train at Sisaket. The train tugged away to Ubon. We said bye to the train and went out of the station. I had already called the friend of mine who regularly took us from Sisaket to my village. It was around sixty kilometres from there.

The car was ready. We put our luggage in, and on the way, we stopped at a gas station. A 7-Eleven store was there. We picked up a few things—some sandwiches, coffee, chocolates, and soft drinks—and we reached home. All my people were there. The minute they saw the car, they rushed, and our luggage was taken to my room. They welcomed him, shook his hands, joked with him, and hugged him. All were talking excitedly, telling him about the function in the temple. There were already people moving in the morning; many were waving at us. They were saying that the function would start in the evening.

In all those three days, nobody would cook at home. Everybody was involved in the temple function. Food, drinks, everything was served in the wat, the temple. We all were there listening to the chanting and watching the ceremony. The monks and many important visitors came and spoke about the goodness of the monk and his contributions to the well-being of the village and to the society.

We were all excited. We settled down in our room.

I told him, 'I'll meet my relatives and come back.'

He said, 'Go ahead. You're with your people. Enjoy it and relax.'

I went to meet my dad and mom. My drunkard brother was already in his seventh heaven, fully drunk. He showed his palm to me.

I told him, 'Not now. You're already drunk. Maybe in the evening, I'll give you money.'

He said, 'No, give me some money.'

I gave him one hundred baht; that was it. Whenever I came, he knew he could take money out of me to buy his booze. I wish he would buy more food instead of booze. It was the curse of the have-nots and maybe the haves—escapism. My dad at this age was doing some work or other. They were trying to be useful; they produced money to take care of the family. Look at the comparison; the son was not bothered. He knew our parents were there to take care of him.

This is where all the problems come from. The rich make money and keep it, so their children don't bother. They don't know the value of money. They don't know how to make money. They don't know and do not believe in hard work. They think that it's available—easy come, easy go. This is the position of a person with more money. For those with little money, they can have a little land, and you work on it. Our children feel we have something. But those who don't have anything, not even a piece of land, they work hard; they know they have nothing else to fall back on. I suppose that is how the whirlpool of life unfolds.

I went back to my room after maybe two, three hours to catch up with my man. I had already sent him a tender coconut and some fruits which he liked. He was comfortable with the air conditioner on. He was reading a book, and he smiled at me.

He asked, 'Are you happy?'

I said, 'I'm very happy. I'm with my people, and I'm looking forward to the festivities and taking the blessings of the dear departed.'

He said, 'Definitely, me too. I look forward to it. We will have a good time with all the people who will be there and the total belief that the monk who is with Buddha will bless all of us. It's an unshakeable faith. They say faith is our god.'

I said, 'What will we eat?'

He said, 'We will wait for dinner.'

I said, 'No, we only had fruits and tender coconut.'

He was smiling. There was a knock. My mother brought food for us; it was spread on the dining table. He once again kissed my mom on the forehead, and she was smiling.

She told him, 'Come and eat.'

He said, 'Yes.'

You know, sign language is beautiful. Everything is done in actions and eye contact. There were many friends and relatives there, and all of us sat and had some rice, fish, and chicken that was available. He took a piece or two. He loved fish and prawns. We quickly ate.

Then I told him, 'I'll meet some of my friends and come back. You take a nap.'

He said, 'Okay.'

Then I went away to catch up with my friends of many years of my childhood. I was radiant, happy, and full of pep, and my family was very happy that I was full of happiness. The irony in life is that the same parents had seen me marry a guy who lived with us for a long time and produce two kids. When he left me, I was alone for many years—nine years. Then suddenly, I found a guy who was showing me so much love, affection, consideration, and giving me a good time in my sexual life also. All these had made me radiant, happy, full of zest in life.

I was with three friends of mine. We were sitting outside, talking about old times. They were asking me about my welfare, whether I was enjoying my life with him. I said, 'It's great.' They were surprised to know that he could perform so well by giving me that kind of sexual happiness. One close friend of mine had lost her husband to another younger woman. An older woman loses to a younger woman. When that younger woman gets old, she will lose to another younger woman. It's a chain reaction that goes on.

She again asked me, 'Are you really enjoying it? Are you making it up to give credit to your guy?'

I said positively, 'Would you like to try it with him?'

She blushed and said, 'No, I don't want to.'

I told them, 'I have to go. He will be waiting.'

They teased me and allowed me to leave them. Believe me, after all my outings, I went back to the room, and he was still reading. My guy read; he loved to read. Of course, he slept, but otherwise, he'd be reading and enjoying himself. He loved the books. I told him I was with three of my friends and that we were talking about sex, life, and how good you are in sex.

Then I mischievously asked him, 'Would you like to have sex with a friend of mine?'

He said, 'What! Definitely not.'

'No? But she does not believe I'm having a good time with you. She thinks you're too old. It's not her fault because generally a man who reaches fifty, drinks too much, works hard, and takes maybe a bit of medicines can't perform. Usually, fifty plus means no sex for the majority of people in the villages. Maybe in the urban areas it's different because they take care of themselves. They have good diet, and they understand the problems of too much drinking and other activities which are bad for the health. But in the villages, the majority loses interest, or they can't perform good sex. And it's a rare phenomenon for them to even have sex once a month. So that friend of mine does not believe me.'

He said, 'Tell her to believe it or forget about it. I will not—'

I said, 'I'm joking. My mom and dad will kill me if they even see anybody going to your room. It is your room now.'

He said, 'Thank you. I don't want anybody else. I'm very happy with you.'

I was feeling great inside. I was pleased. I knew I could believe this guy. As I said, in everybody's life, there will be a good wave to take you to places. Here's a saying: 'You spread your legs according to your bed.' If you spread your legs more, they will be outside the bed, and you'll be uncomfortable.'

So it was the same with my guy. He knew his limitations; he knew it was not that he could have sex with anybody just like that. Maybe if you're really hungry to have sex, any woman or anybody is fine but not on a regular basis. It's like when you have sex today, tomorrow it will be difficult or the next day because you need that kind of adjustment, that kind of understanding with the person with whom you have sex.

I was so happy. I told him to take a shower and get ready to go to the temple.

I said, 'It will be at six o'clock in the evening.'

He said, 'Okay, I'll be ready.'

Then we all got ready. All of us walked to the temple, which was not far from our home. There was music; it was not the normal music that we had at any other function where we danced and all movie songs were played. Here, it was the holy music which was played—live and also recorded. The chants were carried out by the monks. We got into the temple premises, a huge compound. A lot of the areas were covered with temporary roofing. Chairs were put, water was served, soft drinks were being brought out by volunteers as it was hot. In Thailand, most of the time, it is humid and hot except in the winter, when it's cool, very cool.

We went, paid some money, took flowers and incense sticks, and joined the queue. Me and my man walked to the monk who was sitting there. We offered the fruits, flowers, and incense stick to Buddha, and the monk blessed us. Then we knelt down in front of him, and he chanted a few hymns to bless us. We went around the Buddha statue, went back, and passed beneath the casket where the body of the monk was kept on top of a pedestal. We climbed a few steps to look at him and touched the casket in which the body was kept inside. We worshiped, looked at him, asked him for his grace. The body was in perfect condition; it was shrunk, but it looked absolutely great. He was covered by an orange robe, the identity of the monk.

I felt there was some kind of good reaction. Our whole bodies were vibrating inside for me and my guy, I'm sure. He was all serious. The human mind is a mystery. The whole body is created with so many chemicals, and how it reacts to a given situation is a wonder. We both went back and sat in the temple. We were there for quite some time, maybe an hour, and the time passed beautifully. We didn't feel bored. Maybe the young guys went out. They were eating good food, starters, pork, chicken, fish, noodles, and rice. Soft drinks, coffee, and sweets were also available. All were eating and enjoying themselves in the holy premises of the temple.

We then started listening to the chanting. There was a senior monk who was giving a discourse on Buddha. The monk was explaining the many aspects of Buddhism. It was always said that any holy words would have an effect on the humans because any good thought would bring in good vibrations. After an hour or so, there was a final chanting ceremony was performed. A special ceremony was carried out where all the priests who were assembled there were chanting the end hymns. Then finally, the monks started retreating back to their quarters. The crowd was slowly melting down to come back the next day for further ceremonies.

I started slowly walking back with my guy, and then somebody called my name. I was surprised to see a classmate of mine in monk robes.

I was about to say his name, but I controlled myself and said, 'Yes, master.'

With great reverence, he said, 'How are you, and who is this?'

Then I introduced my boyfriend to him. He was speaking very good English, my classmate who had become a monk. I was surprised and asked him with my better English (it was better than my earlier broken English).

I said, 'You speak excellent English.'

He said, 'Yes, I became a monk when I went back from here. After understanding the futility of life, maybe my heart was set to understand the true meanings of life, and I took up the monkhood.'

He had spent many years travelling around Thailand and had visited Cambodia and Vietnam and had also gone to India. So my guy was also a philosopher and knew more about religion, and they both started talking. I was there sitting patiently with my folded hands. We normally wouldn't sit equally with the priest, so we squatted on the floor.

He told me, 'No problem. The function and everything is over. You're my old classmate. Now you have grown big and beautiful. I have grown also by age, but I have yet to learn a lot.'

That was his humility. Then my friend and the monk started talking about religion and especially about Buddhism. In short, they were talking about my friend monk's experiences of understanding the religion and about my guy's experiences in life, having gone deep into knowing most of the religions.

Then the monk said that he had visited Mahabodhi Temple in Bodh Gaya in India, where Buddha attained his nirvana or enlightenment under a pipal tree. My boyfriend said he had also visited that temple. That temple is where all the Buddhists from all over the world, especially from Asia, congregate. They spend many days sitting in front of the pipal tree, chanting, meditating. They visit the temple where Buddha spent many years obtaining nirvana.

They talked about the place my monk friend had visited in Sarnath; that is around two hundred kilometres away from Bodh Gaya near Varanasi, where Buddha gave his first sermon to his disciples. They talked about many things— about the next life, the belief about good karma getting you good results and bad karma getting you bad results. I think all religion say the same, but only in Hinduism and Buddhism do they believe in the incarnation and rebirth till one merges with the god. Christianity and Islam don't believe in rebirth. It's each one's thoughts, but everybody says, 'Do good, be good, and you'll be one with your god. Your life will be full of happiness.'

Maybe after an hour, the monk said, 'I am a little late, but it's okay. We had a nice chat with your guy, and he knows many things. You're lucky to have met him. Maintain your relationship, be happy.' He blessed us, and we prostrated and took his blessings, then we left the temple compound.

We both walked back slowly hand in hand, and my guy said, 'Look at him, this boy when he was young who played hide and seek and all other games with you has become a monk. You have become a massage lady. Look at each one's karma.'

Then I told him, 'You think I'm not doing a very good job?'

He told me, 'Definitely not. You're servicing people. You're removing pain from the body, the physical body of humans, by using your hands, mind, and heart in servicing them. It's a hard work well done.'

'A priest or monk removes the pain in our hearts, in our minds so that we understand the many finer aspects of life and try not to spend or dwell too much in mundane things. It's all going to be enjoyed by me after having accumulated so much, money, land, and wealth.'

He says, 'It's all temporary. It's all transient. You will pass one day, leaving the whole thing for an unknown destination. By any unknown standards, some say you come back, some say you don't come back. It's beside the point. The basic issue remains—anything born has to die. There is a saying that birth is an accident but death is certain.'

Then he stopped. We were almost near our house. My dad, mom, relatives, friends were all sitting. They all called us to sit with them. They were talking to my guy, and he was smiling. He knew only very few words in Thai, and he was trying to say things with his eyes, with his hands, and with the movements of his body. And they were all laughing, smiling. They knew he meant good; he knew they meant good. That was how everybody used the sign language, the universal language of the world.

So it was almost ten in the night, and everybody parted. Normally, as I said earlier, the whole village would sleep by eight o'clock, maximum nine o'clock, even with the advent of TV. This was because they had to get up at five o'clock in the morning to go to the fields by six o'clock and work, but today was an exception because of the temple feast and the monk's anniversary celebration in the wat. We still had to get up early to go back to the temple. The next day, it was my turn to be a volunteer. I had to go early and do a lot of work, maybe help in the cooking or serving water or giving some soft drinks or any other work assigned to me by the leaders of the temple. There was a committee which assigned work to all the people.

So we said goodnight and went into our room, changed, and he just hugged me and said, 'Tomorrow is your D-day to serve the temple. Go to bed and sleep.'

I looked at him, kissed him on his forehead, and said thank you. We both slept, but he was fidgeting; he was not getting any sleep.

Then I asked him, 'What's happening?'

He said, 'Nothing. I'm only trying to understand what happened today in the temple. Look at the dedication of the people who are so much involved in the ceremony to make everybody happy. So this is exactly what community living is. In urban areas, where I hail from, neighbours don't talk to neighbours. They don't even know who lives next to their house or next to their flat, and everybody looks at one another with suspicion, thinking what harm the other person will bring to them.'

In Western countries many people keep guns next to them and sleep, who are they scared of?

I told him, 'Urban life is so different from village life. Here, everybody trusts everybody. Of course, there are many black sheep, but generally, the discipline is well maintained in a village. If you do bad, you'll be removed from the village. Finally, the committees and head man's decision is final.'

He said, 'Fine, you are good at lectures. You will be a head lady one day.'

'I will take it as your blessings and good wishes.'

He slowly held my hand, and we both slowly slipped into a good sleep.

Chapter 17

I got up at six in the morning. I was ready in fifteen minutes. I left word with my mother and my son that they had to take care of my guy. Once he was ready, he could come to the temple. They nodded. I wore my white dress. All volunteers were to wear white dresses to serve in the temple. Generally, for any temple function, all of us would go in white dress. The white colour symbolises purity, divinity and tranquillity.

I went out. There were many of my friends waiting, and we all rushed to the temple. Talking is also like chanting in Thai, so sing-song, so animated. It's very interesting for any foreigner to observe how a Thai person speaks. We reached the temple. Each one was assigned to a work station. I was told to do flower work around the Buddha statue and the body of the monk along with the other five girls. I was very pleased. It was not that I hated cooking—I did love it—but this was more interesting, and it required deft hands to do a little bit of artistic arrangement with the flowers. We had to make it look nice and colourful, and the colour combination should match with the beauty of the Buddha statue and the casket of the monk. We were involved in that work.

By nine o'clock, many people started coming. Chanting was carried out by the monks. The actual program started by nine in the morning when the big priest who had come all the way from Bangkok to perform the ceremony was out from his meditation, and he supervised the celebrations. Everybody held hands for every other chant. When it ended, they had to prostrate with folded hands to the ground, and they should repeat certain verses common for ending a particular stanza for that particular chant. It was very complicated, but that was how we were taught to do it.

Once the ceremony came to an end around ten o'clock, everybody went out and picked up their plates. There was a big queue for food. We all had rice, soup, fish, chicken, pork. We are so habitual; we're all creatures of habit—the same taste and the same food. Anything beyond that or apart from that, you're not satisfied; that's how the human mind or psyche is made. We all ate hungrily, then after my few mouthfuls, I remembered whether my boyfriend had eaten or not.

He was there with his plate. I waved at him. He smiled back, and he was all the time looking at me. He picked up his food and joined me. He loved Thai food, so there was no problem. Anything spicy was what his fare was; of course, he would eat only rice and fish and sometimes a bit of prawns. We ate. All my friends were joking, making fun of us. He understood we were the targets. It was okay; that was how our lives were; it was a pleasure that we were the centre of attraction.

Again after half an hour, at eleven o'clock, there were more chants, more recitations, more rituals, and plenty of incense sticks were burnt. There were holy rhymes sung, and a big lecture was delivered by the chief priest, who talked about the life and achievements of the dead priest. Around twelve thirty, the ceremony came to an end in the afternoon. So we all left. I saw the monk who was my childhood friend; he came and greeted us.

He and my boyfriend and I chatted for some time on general topics. My boyfriend was very pleased to talk to him because that guy understood good English, and they were happy to interact with each other. Then after a little while, we parted for the afternoon siesta. When we started back for home, it was hot. Slowly we came back by another route where there were many trees; we were getting fresh air. We were all totally wet with sweat. We changed, and we watched TV for some time. We felt we could not sleep because our stomachs were half full. Generally, Thais are shy to eat so much in a public function. We had some tender coconuts, fruits, papaya, and soy milk. We have many good things to eat in Thailand—the greens, vegetables, fruits; they are nature's bounty, food in plenty given to us for our nourishment.

Then we both slept for some time. We got up around four thirty after two hours of sleep or so. We took a shower, and we both joined the others for the visit to the temple. There were many musicians who had come from Sisaket. There were many actors and actresses who had come to perform about the life and stories of Buddha. The priest started the function with many recitals, chants, and speeches. Many outside VIPs who had come were all paying their respects, going down and touching the feet of the priests, and taking their blessings. It went on for quite some time, and then food was ready by seven o'clock.

With that break, people started eating. Once everybody's stomach was full, around seven thirty the final ceremony was conducted, and then at nine o'clock, the actors started performing on a stage created for that particular function. Everybody watched. Jokers are part of any function because any serious event requires a break of laughter. Laughter is the one which makes you really get relaxed. All those jokers were creating fun, and everybody was enjoying it. Then there

were many stories of Buddha that were re-enacted. All were
moralistic, trying to make us understand the futility of life
and the merits gained by following the righteous path.

Then by around eleven o'clock, the program ended, and
everybody dispersed back to their homes. We walked back
with so many people from our area. My house was in the
beginning of the entrance of the village. Then inside, there
were many, many houses. Everybody had to pass through
my house, which was on the main street. We said bye to
everybody and then finished our restroom tasks, went back
to our room, and sat down, just holding our hands.

He said, 'It's nice and peaceful. It's nice that people rejoice
in the true things of life. Whatever you believe in, whether
there is a god or not, that's beside the point. Definitely, there
is a god and godliness, which directs our life. Ordinary folks
have hearts that are clean. They do not have any negativity
in them, that kind of greed, too much jealousy, or too much
pride and evil. But the majority struggles to obtain money.
They adopt so many methods, hoping to get lots of money
for them to enjoy. I don't know why, but whatever they earn
and save, they want to enjoy it in one day. Will that one day
may be a mirage, or will they just be accumulating it for
somebody else?'

I understood his point. I told him, 'You're right.'

Then he said, 'Come, let's go to bed. Tomorrow morning
is the final day of the ceremony, the third day, and you'll be
busy.'

I kissed him on the forehead, and he said, 'I would like
to kiss you on the cheeks.'

I said okay. Then I told him, 'Not on my mouth.'

'All ceremonies are part of this body. This body itself is
a temple.'

I told him, 'Yes, you're very right. Let's go to sleep. That's it.'

The final day of the ceremony at the wat was very colourful. A lot of people came from nearby places—from Sisaket, from Pranco, from Khukhan, and so many other places. There was a big crowd. The temple premises was full. Even outside, there were many people waiting to witness the final ceremony. It was a very solemn function where the big priest and other priests were all lined up and many chants and recitals were being conducted. There was many dignitaries who had come from near and far, some even from Bangkok. They all spoke well of the priest, and they said that the same day next year, we'd be cremating the priest. The final decision had to be taken by the committee.

And they all finally closed the ceremony around twelve o'clock. There was a big feast arranged. On the final day, there were a lot of soft drinks and plenty of food, rice, noodles—everything. It was a feast fit for the aristocracy. Everybody had their stomachs full and were mighty happy. Food is the only thing people say, 'Enough, enough,' but for all other needs, we say, 'Give me more, more.' The ceremony was over; everybody was chanting. The priest's body, which was placed outside the temple for all of us to view, was shifted back into the temple. It had to rest for one more year before the final journey to cremation, from ashes to ashes. Then the temple doors were closed with more chanting, and the final ceremony came to an end. So we bid farewell to my childhood friend, the priest or monk, who was going back to Bangkok the next day to pursue his future career. My boyfriend talked to him for some time, then we returned back home.

On the way back, we took a detour and went to see our land. My parents, my relatives, my drunkard brother were all happy with their eating and drinking. All were pleased to see us looking at the land, and I was making my man understand all the things we intended to do in the course of time. We wanted to develop the land and add some fruit-giving trees. Growing lemon trees was a big business now because lemon was very expensive. Then I was talking about my plans of developing a piggery since the pig business is a big business in Thailand.

In the hot sun, we slowly walked back to our room, to our home. We were totally wet with sweat, so we took a shower, went back, and settled down.

I told him, 'I'll go to my mother's house and come back.'

He said, 'Fine.'

I told him, 'Lie down and relax for some time. I'll join you later.'

He said, 'Okay.'

I smiled at him, and I kissed him on his lips. He was looking at me with awe. I told him, 'You're now free. The three-day ceremony is finished. You're now a free man to do what you like.'

He was all excited. He said, 'Come now.'

I said, 'I'll come back. You relax for some time.'

Then I went back to see my dad and mom at their place. My mom was the big boss of the house, and there were many other relatives from far and near who had come for the ceremony at the temple. They were all saying bye, and everybody wanted to say bye to my guy. I called him to come and bid farewell to our relatives. He rushed to join me in my dad's house. From my house, my mom's house was two houses away. In the middle was my aunt and uncle's house. They said bye, and everybody left.

My mom said, 'Go and sleep for some time. Your man looks tired.'

I said, 'No problem. Thank you.'

We went back to our room, closed the door, and we were hugging each other. We slowly removed our clothes, but there was an urgency to it. Three nights of abstinence, one night in the train and two nights here—three nights and four days; sex was on! It was okay; we were committed to a program.

There are many who never get this opportunity in life as sex is only the second hunger. The first hunger is taken care of, and when you have a higher joy, that was the worship or the activity at the temple. There is merit in attending to that particular work. So you drop your lower joy to attain a higher joy. Not that I think about it, sex is a lower joy. Everything has got a yard stick. Sex is a medium to achieve oneness with the maker of this universe. But priorities give numbers to your needs.

In Pattaya we were focused on sex, so till then, we were busy; that was the priority. Then when we travelled by train, no activity; it was more of a public place. The next day at home, there were the holy ceremonies. So the priority was attending to the temple chores and attending to the people who had come to visit us. It is nothing but your mental adjustments giving priorities. What is first? What is second? What is third? That's how you have to understand. Certain things you'll have to control. You'll have to tell yourself yes or no, and you have to give importance to that. It's not that it's programmed; it is spontaneous. But of course, there are certain parameters you have to follow.

We had given preference to other things. Now all that was over, and we were back to ourselves. Let's call it back to our nature. We were pagans. We were totally naked. Then we were hungry. We both were kissing, licking, touching. I was on him; he was on me. We had our sixty-nine; he had mine in his mouth, and I had his in my mouth. We were eager and greedy. It went on for quite some time. We were busy sucking and nibbling at each other. After ten minutes, he kept on relentlessly working on my clitoris and my vagina. And I was licking his balls or his testicles and his penis. We both were about to cum in each other's mouths.

He hurriedly moved, and I adjusted myself to the top position. Then we both moved together, and he was in my vagina. I was pumping, and he was also matching me. And then it was a big explosion which initially started well and ended in a beautiful way. We had such a big orgasm. His semen was pouring out, and my cum was coming out. We both were very, very happy. Our lips were locked, and we were holding each other tight. We were two bodies which had become one. We were like that for quite some time. Where was the hurry? We could always take it out.

And we always had a small game. He tried to tickle me from inside. I tried to close my vagina. It's an exercise which is part of the Kegel exercise to control your muscle tissues and to make them stronger. So you make the movements without any restrictions to the best of your capacity. We were like that for quite some time, then he started losing his erection, and I was almost full with liquid in my vagina. Once I removed myself from him, the whole thing poured on to his penis. I took a tissue and cleaned him up. I was also holding on to my vagina, and I cleaned up myself.

Still we were in my home, and there was no attached bathroom. It was the same bedroom where I had my first encounter with my husband. Thoughts of my first night with that guy came to me. He had not come to the wat for the ceremony this time because he knew that I would be coming with my boyfriend. So then I cleaned myself. I got my towel. I opened up the door. No one was there, and I went into the bathroom.

We both slept for some time, maybe an hour or so. We were contented and pleased with ourselves. We got ready after a shower and decided to go for a walk. On the way, we went into my uncle's house. He was a rich man, my dad's cousin brother. He had a very big house and had all the goodies a rich man would have in his house. Now, even an ordinary man has a refrigerator, a TV; they're part of Westernization. At my uncle's house, we chatted for some time with his sons and daughters. They also spoke a little bit of English.

One of the daughters and my guy talked about general issues of the world. She explained about the agricultural activity, having water, and at the same time, dependence on rains—that was where all our problems came in, and for agriculturists who did not have big lands, they couldn't sustain themselves if the rains did not come. My guy said that we should do cottage industries.

In Asia, most of the poor countries depend on rain for their crops. With the promotion of the garment industry in Asia, a lot of new cottage industries connected with villages are being promoted. There are many—candle making and making of paper mash toys—and there are other activities wherein you can produce handicrafts. You can make many Thai heritage products, which are accepted and are liked by the tourists who throng the big cities of Thailand. The village committees can take up this kind of work and try to build and give work to the guys who do not have enough work whenever the agricultural activity is not available. They can be usefully employed, and they can earn a certain amount of money. It will be useful for them for their day-to-day use. Most of them don't have to pay any rent because they have a small piece of land where they have a ramshackle house or a wooden house or maybe a good brick-and-mortar house. But the main problem is their day-to-day expenses. They need gas for cooking. They need vegetables, grains, spices, and non-vegetarian items, like pork, chicken, fish, and all that. They also need money for electricity, water, education, health, and entertainment.

So we spent maybe two, three hours. They offered us dinner. We said that Mummy would be waiting for us at home. We took some soft drinks, but my guy didn't drink that, so a tender coconut was given to him. They were ready to offer some whiskey or beer. He politely refused, and we went back home. Then we had our dinner at home, our most lovable tom yam pla, fish in spicy soup, which is loved by my guy, the spicy one which contains plenty of greens. We have green vegetables, mushrooms, and a lot of spicy food in Thailand. Pork was there, which I took, but my guy didn't eat pork because it contained more fat. We finished our food and chit-chatted for some time as we were to leave the next day back to Pattaya.

We bid bye to my people and went back to our room. We watched TV for some time. My son talked about his football matches, and my brother's daughter, who also lived in our house as her parents lived in Bangkok for their work, talked about her school.

As we were talking, my guy said, 'I'll go and read a book.' I said, 'Fine, go ahead.'

Then I spent more time with the children, talking to them, as I was leaving the next day by noon to catch a direct bus from Sisaket to Pattaya. Otherwise, we would have to take a train to Bangkok, and then we'd have to take a bus from Bangkok to Pattaya. The bus was the most luxurious one; it had totally reclining seats. Of course, my guy didn't like bus journeys, but once in a while, he was game; he would adjust to the circumstances. I said goodnight to my children. They went away to their granny's house to sleep, and I bolted the door.

I went into our room, and he was reading. I asked him what it was about. He said, 'Philosophy.'

I told him, 'Again philosophy?'

'Yes, life is nothing but philosophy. It is the driving force of all life.'

'Okay, let me listen to it.'

He told me there was a lady with a child whom she loved so much. It was the apple of her eye, but one day, it got fever and died. She was totally upset; she was totally shattered. She didn't know what to do. She carried the child and rushed to the monk who was sitting beneath a tree. That was Lord Buddha.

She put the child at his feet and said, 'My lord and master of this universe, please bring my child back to life. You can perform many miracles. Please give me back my child. I want my child. I don't want anything else. Take my life, but I want my child to live.'

Buddha smiled and said, 'Okay, Kisa Gauthami.' That was her name. 'Please go to any of the houses nearby and ask for a handful of sesame seeds. You can accept them only on the condition that there should have been no death in that house.'

The lady said, 'Okay, it's easy. I will come back in a jiffy. Take care of my child.'

Buddha said, 'My child, don't worry, I will take care of your child.'

She rushed to the nearest house and knocked. The lady of the house opened the door and asked, 'What? What happened? What do you want?'

She said, 'Ma'am, my son has died, and Buddha said he will bring him back to life, but he wants a handful of sesame seeds. Please give some to me.'

'Oh, that's not a problem. I will go bring it.'

'But, ma'am, in your house, nobody should have died.'

She said, 'Sorry, last month my dad passed away.'

'Oh my god, I'll try next door.' She kept on going from house to house, asking for a handful of sesame seeds with the condition. Everybody had a story to tell; brother, mother, father, uncle, son, husband—in every house, there was death. She must have gone to hundreds of houses, but every house had death.

She went back, shattered, to Buddha and said, 'Master, what is this? I can't find a single house where there is no death.'

The master smiled and told her, 'This is the true meaning of life, my dear child. Death is part of life. You can't escape it. You are bound by it. Don't worry about anything else. Live today and enjoy the beautiful things given by godliness. When death comes, accept it slowly and happily. That's how life goes on.'

My guy smiled at me and said, 'You know, this story is very famous. You are a Buddhist. I am not. I knew the story, but you did not. Maybe you had no time or nobody had told you. Maybe people have more learning opportunities in urban areas.'

I told him, 'It's a nice story, and I'll share it with many others.'

He told me, 'There are many other stories, but I was reading something else connected to it, more philosophy. I gave you just the basic in a story form for you, so that you will appreciate it.'

I said, 'I do appreciate it. I understand death is a beautiful thing to happen.'

He told me, 'It's only a change of clothes. You get into your new clothes for your new dreams, a new life. So do not worry over or fear death. Accept it with a smile when it comes to you.'

That was how he finished the story, and he was smiling at me. We talked for quite some time. I told him about my dreams of making more money.

He said, 'Yes, it is a nice thing that you want to produce more wealth. It's good for you, good for your village, and good for the whole country. All should work hard to earn money, but in the process, you should not get burnt out.'

I told him, 'Yes, definitely, I will not. I have my targets. Once I reach those targets, I will give up.'

'Let's see,' he told me. 'You have ambition. You want to go up in life. You want to make your family happy, your children happy, your relatives, friends, and everybody. It's a very noble thought, and I appreciate the great cooperative movement you always have here. But you should understand there is divine intervention or an unknown hand which holds your finger and leads you to your destination. You will appreciate now that you're working with a boss and that you don't know at all what will unfold in your life. What you think is great today may not be great in the course of time. What you think is not good may be very good at a later stage. Basically, life is in motion. Life is a duality. Life has a yin and yang. It's always has two faces. And as you grow, you'll understand.

You should and must take care, know your limitations, try
to plan, and follow a set goal with all your fervent prayers to
your god.' Or he called it godliness.

I told him, 'Fine.'

He told me, 'The day is followed by night, and then it is
followed by day. So you can say day, night, and day. So there
are two days and one night and two nights and one day. That
is the duality. That is how life is to be understood. If there is
rain, there is sunshine. Today, who doesn't have a problem?
Each one has different kinds of problems. Who does not
have pain in their hearts? Everybody has got pain in their
hearts. Some share, some don't share, but it is there. People
do not know how exactly for them to conduct themselves
because it's human nature to cry when you're sorrowful and
to laugh out when you're happy. We are all pawns in the game
of some higher power, whom we call god or godliness. We
bow our heads down and pray and seek solace, happiness,
and peace.'

I said, 'Yes, whatever you say is right. Everybody has
got problems. I have problems. I have pain. But now it is all
settled, and I'm doing well.'

I have my dreams, and I'm very confident about my hard
work. The support of my family, the support of you and my
boss, my good karma, the blessings of Buddha will take me
to places.'

He said, 'Absolutely, you're on the right path.'

Our conversation sort of came to an end, and we let our
thoughts lie low. We both settled down. He was holding
me. I was pulled to his chest, and it was very peaceful. We
slowly melted into each other, and we fell asleep. Then in the
middle of the night, maybe it was around two o'clock, there

was a small movement, and he moved away from me. Then I was awakened and went for my nature's call and came back.

I was contemplating. I was thinking that what was waiting for me was a bright future. Now I had gotten out of my shackles of being bound to a marriage which got broken. Now I was earning as a massage lady, and I had my ambitions to do well. I was thinking, then he stirred; I just tickled him up, and he was wide awake.

I told him, 'Go to the bathroom.' He slowly got up, and he finished his job and came back to the room. He was looking at me. There was some small light coming from the window; it was falling on my face, and I was smiling. Then he came and sat next to me and started kissing me. I responded. We both were happy to be together. Then the process of body movements started.

He started moving all over me. I responded with equal fervour. We both were eager for each other's bodies and the process of having a good time. A good sex act started. He got into me straight, and then he was moving. I was moving. Then he made me turn to his favourite position of me becoming a doggy and him becoming a male doggy; he started moving. This particular position gave full penetration; our movements were easier, and then it gave us more excitement. He kept on moving, then again I told him, 'Let's change.' I came on top of him. He was holding on to my breast, and he was making all kinds of circles; he was moving his fingers expertly. I was moving on him, and it became a beautiful rhythm.

We both were almost ready, and then he said, 'You want me to come on top?'

I said, 'No, you stay where you are.'

Then I kept on pumping, and he kept on arching and moving into me. Then we both came. It was a big and nice finish, and we were totally spent. Then we stayed for some more time like that, and I withdrew. We were happy, and every time we finished, we would have that feeling of oneness with the power which produced us.

I keep on saying it a number of times; it's one of the greatest happiness the power has created in the universe and has gifted to humans. I pray and wish that everybody in this world who has not gone through the sex act would get this moment of happiness in all their lives. The rhythm and understanding between a man and a woman should be savoured, should be felt, and the patience of both bodies to give and take will only bring in that kind of happiness.

We relaxed, looking at each other, again kissing, and we were not talking. We were each looking at each other's faces for the reaction.

Finally, my superman said, 'How happy life is, how unhappy it can become. How can I make it always happy for us and for everybody?'

Then with my knowledge, I said, 'It's not in our hands, but let's try to do what we can do so that everybody can be happy.'

Then he talked about my uncle's daughter saying that there was no income for the people in the village when there was no agricultural activity. Then he said, 'We should plan for some activities for a cottage industry. In their free time, they can do some work to produce handicrafts which can be sold in the market.'

I agreed with him and said, 'We will try to find out how best the government can also support this program for villages. These are normally available in the social welfare ministry. We keep on feeling for others. It's a nice thing not to always think about ourselves. It's a good thing to think about others also.'

We slipped back to our sleep, and when we got up in the morning, it was almost eight o'clock. We were up, got ready after a shower, and had a good breakfast of tender coconuts, fruits, and pastries. I know my guy didn't like pastries, but I had bought them from 7-Eleven—some pies and some bread. Again he did not like to eat rice in the morning. I had my rice, soup, pork; that was our staple food. Once we finished our breakfast, we both went back to the wat (that is, the temple) to take the blessings of the departed revered priest whose body was resting in the casket near the Buddha statue for one more year.

We were there to catch up with my friend monk, who was leaving for Bangkok for his seminary or to his wat, the temple where he would take care of his flock of devotees. We said goodbye and then prayed once again and took the blessings. Then on the way, I saw a few of my friends. I bid farewell to them, saying that by afternoon we would be going back to Pattaya. They said, 'Take care.' And then we went back home.

So by one o'clock, there was a farewell feast with rice, fish, prawns, and mushrooms. We had green curry, red curry, and some tom yam soup. We had our fill. I told my parents, 'I'm happy going back to work. Bless us. Any blessings from elders are good for us so that I do well in my life.'

They said bye, and we got into a taxi and went to Sisaket. Our bus was waiting, and we got into it.

Chapter 18

The journey was a little tedious for him, but I was used to it. For any night journey, you have to sit, stretch 180 degrees, and maybe turn around, but still it's not like lying down flat on a bed. We reached Pattaya early in the morning, maybe at four o'clock. We went to the hotel, checked in, and slept for some time. We got up in the morning and had breakfast in the hotel.

I told him, 'I'll go report to my work and to my boss.'

He said, 'Fine.'

Then I went and said hello to my friends and to my boss. My boss was smiling and said, 'You had a nice holiday in your home with your boyfriend?'

I said, 'Yes, thank you. I had a very good time.'

She said, 'Nice, start your work.'

Then I said, 'Today I won't be working. I'll be with him because he'll be leaving tonight back to his place. So tomorrow, I'll start working.'

She said, 'Fine, no problem. Go ahead and have a good time.'

I went back to him. He was happy, and then we went out to Big C, a big supermarket in Pattaya where you get all the things you require. It was a common man and rich man's joint where you get all the things in one store—the day-to-day things, anything you might need, clothing, perfume, food, fruits, groceries, all the things that a household would need. He bought a few things to take with him. He said, 'Buy what you want for yourself.' I picked up a few toilet items, and then we bought some doughnuts, the hot, hot ones for our afternoon brunch. We had finished our breakfast, of course, and the dinner would be around seven o'clock. Then he would leave for the airport. We went back to the room. Maybe it was one o'clock; it was hot outside. We ate the doughnuts and went to bed.

I wondered at how every day is basically the same. Only situations and circumstances change. You get up, eat, work, eat, work, eat, and sleep after a bit of recreation. In a village, you have a lot of talking, but again it's the same thing: work, talk, work, talk. Even in the city, it's the same. But you see, it varies. There's not much of—what should I say?—make-believe assumptions, whereas in a city you have to have a lot of etiquette, a lot smiles. When you look at a person, you have to smile; it has to come spontaneously. Spontaneity is the answer to making yourself happy as life is such a beautiful thing. We do enjoy being involved in some kind of activity wherein you help somebody who needs your support; it makes you really happy. So it is said that in giving, you find more happiness, and in helping, you find more happiness.

Then my guy said, 'I'm going today. I will come back after three months. I will miss you a lot. Be a good girl and take care of yourself.'

I said, 'Fine. Three months will pass in a jiffy. I will concentrate on my work. You concentrate on your work, and we wait for our meeting after three months.'

He said, 'This should be our motto. In the beginning of our relationship, I was going away with so much of sadness. I used to be worked up. Now we have settled down to a pattern, and that's it. There's no issue.'

We both were eager to be together as that day was the last opportunity to have good sex, so we intended to make it the best. We peeled off our clothes, had a shower together, helped each other in doing all the rubbings in the water. He sucked my tits. My nipples were hard. My breasts were swelling. I was all hot and ready. He made me bend and asked me to hold on to the bathtub; I was almost in an L shape. He entered my vagina from the rear, which he loved (me too), because his testicles and upper thighs would hit me hard on my buttocks and his strong, erect penis moving inside me would make me feel great. Then he was pumping me, hitting me hard, and he was changing directions. It was a gyration, a movement, a belly dance.

Then after five minutes or so, he was physically tired. I was not. He was standing, and then he made me turn. I told him it would be better if he lay down on the floor of the bathtub. He was slightly elevated because of the curve of the bathtub, and I let him enter me. That was the best position in the bathroom. I was on him, moving; he was moving. The water was sloshing around us. It was a nice experience. Warm water was all over us, and our bodies were moving. It went on for a few minutes, and finally, we both had a great finish. He ejaculated, his semen coming out, and I had an orgasm, a big one. I was in ecstasy, and he was also shouting out, saying, 'It was great!'

We stayed for some more time, and then I withdrew from him. We continued our shower, cleaned ourselves, and then we came out of the bathtub, dried each other, and then got ready. We both left for our usual joint for our dinner, a little early as he was to leave by seven o'clock. We went back to our room. He had so much mixed feelings. He was sad that he was going to miss me, and at the same time, any parting brought a lot of vigour and happiness for when we would meet again. We passionately hugged each other and kissed for a long time. There was affection in it instead of sex.

We called the bellboy. His luggage was brought down and loaded into the waiting taxi. He waved at me, went out of the car, kissed me, hugged me, and said bye. Then he left—to come back in three months.

He left for the airport to go back to his surroundings. I went back to my work station, to my shop, and reported back to duty. Instead of going in the morning of the next day, I thought, *What will I do alone?* There were many customers; all the five girls were busy working. One more customer came in. My cashier said, 'You're willing to work?' I said yes, and I took the job. I smiled at the customer, a European. I did a foot massage, and he was a very tired old man. I took good care of him, and he was very pleased. He almost slept during the one-hour process, and he was virtually snoring. I didn't disturb him for as long as possible. And I did a very light kneading and squeezing of his muscles, and his legs were beautifully responding. And his foot was so delicate. He woke up from his sleep, and then he gave a satisfied smile. He thanked me and gave me a good tip and then went away. Again on a rotation basis, in my turn I had a wonderful opportunity for an oil massage.

Many people come late in the night—that is, after eleven o'clock—visiting hot tourist spots, visiting sex shows; they get excited. They are new to the culture of the East; the Europeans and Americans are fascinated by it. We get a lot of groups from Vietnam, Cambodia, Laos, and others from all over Asia. People come to Thailand, especially to Pattaya, where we have a variety of live shows.

Now I had an Asian who had come for an oil massage. I started massaging him. He was a middle-aged guy; he was relaxing. He was looking at me when he was on his back. His English was broken English, and mine was better now. He had a small erection when I was feeling him on his thigh and stomach portion of the oil massage. His eyes were intent, and he was hesitant. Maybe I took the cue, but I didn't speak because there was a thin screen separating us from the other bed, where the other massage was on.

I made the sign of shaking a bottle of cola. He nodded. Yes. I showed my fingers, five fingers. He nodded in affirmation, and then I told him to pay for the action. His pants and shirt were all next to him. He took out his purse and paid me the five hundred baht. I told him to relax, and I started removing his towel, which covered his manhood. We normally had a towel, a new towel, given to the client for the oil massage. Initially, the customer would lie face down, and we would complete the back, the neck, the buttocks, the back of the thighs, the calf muscles, and the foot. That took around thirty minutes. Then we would ask them to lie down on their back, and then we'd massage the chest and the stomach. Of course, we never go to the main point, only up to the thigh point and then down to the leg, and we'd then complete the oil massage in one hour.

Forty-five minutes had almost been completed. I had another fifteen minutes left to complete the massage. All of us used the towel to cover the back and buttocks when we did it from the rear, and when he was on his back, his penis and testicles were covered by the towel. Only for a happy ending did we remove the towel. I removed the towel in anticipation that his erection was better. He had a small penis, maybe four inches; maybe when it became fully erect, it could be five or more.

I slowly started moving my hands. He had some pubic hairs. I was feeling his testicles or the balls. Slowly my hand cupped his manhood. He was wriggling, and he was excited. I asked him, 'What all the shows you saw?'

He said he went to the Alcazar show, saw so many beautiful girls, then took a walk, saw many tourists, and he was all excited. I asked him whether he had come alone. He said he was in a group, and his wife was with all the ladies and had gone out shopping. I said, 'Okay, let me complete it.' It took five minutes, and when I knew he was about to come, the towel was handy. I took all his semen in it, and I kept on shaking it; he was very pleased. He was hugging himself, and he tried to touch my thighs, which we normally didn't mind. He was holding on till his ejaculation was complete.

He was all apologetic, and he was nice. I told him to relax, then I completed the final phase of making him sit down on the bed and doing a bit of massage for the neck and for the shoulders and slight movements on the hips. Then I tapped him three times on the back, and then I said, 'That's it.' I allowed him to get up and dress. He finished dressing. He came out and paid the cashier for the massage. Then he paid me a two-hundred-baht tip; that was generous of him. He said to me, 'Kha pun khap.' That is thank you in Thai, and I reciprocated with a bow to him.

I was richer by five hundred for the happy ending, the two-hundred-baht tip, and my share of the massage, which was one hundred, so that was eight hundred baht. The other massage brought in another one hundred as my share, and with the one-hundred-baht the tip, it became one thousand baht; that was thirty US dollars, the money earned for two hours of my work. My hands were the ones which held many people's futures, and also it held my future. I had to take care of my hands, and you know, we were a tired lot.

Any girl in need of a massage would ask another girl to do a massage for her. And we normally gave fifty baht as a tip for the services; nothing was free. Of course, the boss would not get anything; it was the staff's services. There was some kind of understanding; sometimes, some girls would refuse the payment, and we would still say, 'Keep it, and buy something for yourself.' No one wanted a free service. We were not greedy for one another's money. We wanted to work hard and earn our money. That was told by my boyfriend, again I had to bring him in, because he was always in me, my mind, my body, and my soul.

Big business guys make millions in a day. How do they make it? All manipulation. The whole issue is, how can they manipulate? There's a name for that; it's called business. In business, everything is fine. You get a contract to make a big building, and you get a quote, a quote for billions of dollars. In the billions, maybe material costs are major, and the labour cost is also a good amount. But the labourers are squeezed. Now there are a lot of mechanical innovations; it's all mechanized. People are not needed in many of the industries. People are jobless. They run to do any kind of work for any amount of money. The shots are called by the guys who make the big money. That's how big guys, big companies make millions of dollars. It's business. The share market, the business is done like that.

In this trade, I could make a thousand baht if I put in two hours. But a physical labourer in a village, even with a whole day's work (for ten hours of hard work), could earn only three hundred baht; that was the comparison. In the hospitality industry, one can make so much more. But the same guy in Bangkok in a job where he's doing manipulation or adjustments can make big money. It is because he's educated. He's learned the trade, and he can earn that kind of money. See the methods? I won't call them anomalies, but that's how I think life has been made from time immemorial. That is what is being done. There are always classes from top to bottom. I don't know why the maker has done all these things. I suppose, the maker enjoys doing this. Maybe variety is the spice of life.

I was working with total dedication. I wanted to make money, so I had to get involved deep in the job. It is the finest massage that can bring you repeat customers. There are many guys, whether it's male or female, who come for a massage and are totally involved in getting their body pain, their discomforts eased out by a proper massage.

Chapter 19

I had one customer, an American, maybe forty-five years old. He was staying in the hotel where the massage shop was located. He came for a massage to the shop. There were five girls, including me, the sixth. Whenever there was a good crowd, we had six masseuse, but if the crowd was less, two girls would go to the other shop—managing labour for optimum utilization.

So this guy wanted me to massage him; they got the right to choose the girl. He wanted an oil massage. I gave him a clean towel, told him to change, and get into his birthday suit. He smiled, and he was a little surprised to hear me speaking tolerable English. Now I'd learned from my guy. I had a bit of an accent when speaking to Americans or Europeans. It was all part of the training, or you could call it tricks of the trade.

Then I closed the screen for him. I asked him, 'Are you ready?' I had already told him to lie face down on the pillow. I went in, told him to relax. 'First, I'll be doing a gentle massage from head to toe.' He said, 'Okay.' Then he lay down. I started methodically working from his head, ears, and on the neck portion, which we did very slowly in a particular movement with the thumb going in circles, up and down, and going down through the shoulders to the hand. So the nerves, the frayed nerves, would be relaxed. I started applying oil slowly on to his back, and he was slowly relaxing his body.

We would normally repeatedly tell the customer to relax. 'Please relax so you'll get the best benefit of the massage.' He was relaxing, and I was massaging him by applying the Johnson's Baby Oil. We had an American product, I suppose. All were treated as babies when we did the massage. So both my hands were moving fast, quickly, efficiently, relieving his pain from his back, shoulders, and lower back. The towel was moved a little down for me to get to his back for the massage, for it to be treated nicely. Then I moved the towel up, and his buttocks were massaged; here we would use a little more pressure because it was a mass of flesh that was to be nicely treated for it to be relaxed. It took so much load when we spent so many hours sitting while doing our work or travelling; it needed the relaxation. And then I went down to his thighs, the back of his thighs, then his knees, his calf muscles, ankles, then to the feet, and all the toes. We would keep on applying the oil and relaxing the muscles.

He was happy. He said, 'Can this be done for two hours?'

I said, 'Yes, sir. Why not?' Then I opened the screen and told my cashier it would be a two-hour massage.

She smiled and said, 'Okay.'

Then I told him, 'I will take more time on the back because it is for two hours.'

He said, 'As you wish, I'm feeling good.'

Then I continued to do a more intense massage on his back. The back had so many concentrated nerves. We were not doctors, and we didn't know much, but we'd been taught by our teachers how we should do the massage without damaging or without stressing the nerves of the body. There were many pressure points where we could give more pressure for the circulation to improve. Then I made him turn around.

Normally, in a one-hour massage, for half an hour, they couldn't look at me because they would be facing the bed. But they would turn in the other half hour, and when they were on their back, they could look at me and speak to me; that was the time when everything would happen.

He was relaxed. I think his penis was limp. We girls always had this curiosity. When we touched the guy in the right places, he would get an erection. We sometimes did it intentionally, normally it is unintentional. We would move our hands, and the fingers could touch the penis or the testicles of a man. It could touch the vagina and some portions of a woman when we massaged a female. It was part of the moment. It was not a machine; the hands were at work.

This guy's penis was limp. Then I started working on his chest, on his hands, and on his stomach. The stomach portion of the massage was very important, and we had to do it very carefully because we would use clockwise and anticlockwise movements so that the stomach area was nicely moved. I moved my fingers, made the towel go down; still there was no reaction in him. Then I started using my fingers on his thighs and went down slowly to the knee portion, and then of course, down to the foot. It was fast, quick, good, strong movements. He was enjoying the strong pressing of his flesh, and he was happy; there was a look of gratitude. Of course, I wouldn't call it gratitude, but there was a look of happiness in his eyes. He was enjoying the massage. I continued to work on him. I had finished one and half hours. There was another half an hour left, so I was moving on to him.

He told me slowly, 'Can you take a look at my friend?' I did not understand at first. In a split second, I understood he meant his penis as his 'friend'. I smiled, and it was almost a laugh, but I controlled it. Then he took from the pocket of his dress, which was there next to him, a five-hundred-baht note and put it in my hand. I said okay. I removed the towel; his tool or penis was limp. I had learned in this little period of experience. There were only one or two cases where there was absolutely no erection when I did an oil massage. And they never bothered to explain nor did I ask them for the reasons. It was understood that they couldn't get an erection because they had erectile dysfunction. I smiled at him and told him to relax. I took some oil and started applying it on his penis, on his testicles, and on his thighs, and slowly I started massaging him. I was trying to tickle him up; yes, he was getting tickled, but there was no erection.

I wondered about the maker's plans, the maker's ingenuity in making some big tools and some small ones. That is life—again, the reality. It may not be a correct explanation or a comparison; maybe it can be compared.

I started using both my hands, putting a lot of oil. I was trying to feel him. I started feeling beneath his testicles; that's where the G point for a man is located. I told him to raise his legs up a little and stretch them a little more so that I could feel the area between his thighs, the testicles, and the point of the anus. So I applied more oil. I started massaging him slowly and steadily and trying to use all the knowledge, whatever had been taught to me by my teachers in trying to rejuvenate him. Maybe the problem had been with this guy for quite some time.

So I started honestly; I even prayed to Buddha to give this man whatever he had lost, to at least let him enjoy a little more in his life. And then there was a small, very small movement, and his penis just moved a little. The guy's eyes were wide open; he must have been closing it. I looked at him, and there was a small movement. Then I kept on working on the finer points of his G spot. And then there was some kind of better movement than the earlier one. So I kept on using one hand to try to prop him up; the penis needed support just to come out from its inside sheath. He was mighty pleased. There was a bit of movement. Then he was all excited. 'Aha!' And he was smiling. And then it was almost two hours, and we got a reminder by the cashier by saying it was time. Then we understood that time was up. Everybody understood. Then I tried to move a little more on his penis. There seemed to be some kind of small movement. He was happy.

I told him and looked at him quizzically.

Then he said, 'Can you come to my room for a massage?'

I said, 'Yes, I can.'

He said, 'Thank you.' Then he dressed, went out, paid the money for the massage to the cashier, and tipped me five hundred baht; it was a big one. All the girls were looking with open eyes.

Then he said to the cashier, 'Can I call this lady to my room later?'

She said, 'Yes.' She knew little English.

He said, 'Okay, thank you.' Then he went away.

All the girls were saying, 'What happened? And what did you do, a happy ending?'

I said, 'No.'

We didn't hide anything from our colleagues because it was part of the job. It was the spice; it cut the monotony from the work we did. Each one commented, compared, and passed good, bad, or ugly remarks depending on the customers. Some were bad guys who were rude. Then of course, some of them were sweet and good, and we praised them. That's human nature.

I was tired. I went out to the 7-Eleven shop which was outside our hotel and picked up a Vita bottle. Vita is a drink, not a fizz drink; it's made from the pulp of a berry fruit. There are many types of Vitas. You get chicken, bird, bird's egg, berries, blueberries, and many other fruits. These are concentrated, extracted, put in a small bottle, and it's supposed to give you more energy and strength. We would drink it when we were tired to make us ready for more assignments.

I went back to my work station after two, three hours; it was maybe nine o'clock in the night. The phone rang; the cashier attended to it. All girls were eager for business. As I told you, whenever the phone rang, mostly it was a demand of a customer in the hotel room for a massage girl to go and do a massage, etc. So the lady spoke. She noted down the room number, and then she said, 'Yes, okay.' Then she looked at me and said, 'Your American guy wants you. It's a two-hour massage.'

Then I smiled, held my coat (the white one), took my tools of the trade, and went to the room of the guy. I boarded the lift, got out at the third floor, and looked for the room number. I knocked, and he was there. He welcomed me, and then I told him to undress. I put a towel on the bed so that the oil wouldn't go on to the bed; that was the instruction given to us by the hotel management. I told him to lie down. I knew exactly why he had called me. He wanted to continue that act where his penis could get an erection, the million-dollar question. He wanted to see those moments of his penis moving on its own. It was nothing but the blood supply that needed to be improved so that the blood would rush into those veins and he'd gets an erection. He now wanted a small erection at least. I started massaging him on the finer points of where I had left in the evening—his G spot. There was a definite improvement in that small erection. I kept on feeling him slowly. He wanted to touch me. I told him, 'Go ahead, no problem.' It was part of my trade. He had already given me the right amount of money. I could feel that the guy was a gentleman, so there was no problem.

He felt my breasts slowly, and he wanted me to open up, to remove my coat, my T-shirt, and my bra so that my breasts could be seen. He started slowly feeling them. I started feeling his testicles, working slowly on his penis. He was moving his legs. There was definitely a reaction; one which was coming externally from my hand and the other coming from his insides. He must have had that reaction, that expectation, the new feel of touching an Asian woman or a different woman from his own stock, not a white woman. I have a white complexion but an Asian.

He was getting that kind of excitement slowly. His face was red. He was happy. His hands became a little hard on my breast; of course, he was not hurting me, just trying to feel my nipples. My nipples reacted to his touch by becoming hard and big. Surprisingly, I was not panting; my mind was focused on the work. I didn't react, but my body reacted, and my mind did not react.

The mind is the one that controls the whole system. It comes by practice. If you meditate, if you control your thoughts, you can't react to this kind of external stimuli. Of course, the stimuli and the response are natural. But if you double up the resistance to a particular level by practice, you can control it to a very great extent; that is how you can block those thoughts. The monks do many things. They're without food and water for many days and many weeks, months, and years. There are many saints who were monks who have cultivated this kind of practice to control the emotions.

But my body reacted. My breasts had become big; my nipples were hard. He was getting excited. He was happy. He was panting, and he was having a better erection. The limpness had changed to a little erection. There was a kind of movement going on in his body. He was all moving. His legs were making a lot of movements, and he was making sounds. It was maybe in his mind that he was having a sexual encounter with a female. Maybe in his mind, he was having a session, an intercourse. That small erection lasted maybe for five minutes, and he suddenly stopped moving his hands on my breast. He was tired, exhausted, and he was breathing heavily. He had closed his eyes. I allowed him to have that pleasurable moment, I guess, for him to savour it. I got up from there and went and sat on a chair in the room.

The guy came back to his normalcy maybe in ten minutes, then he got up, got dressed, and put on his shorts and a T-shirt. He came and sat on another chair opposite to me, and he started talking to me. He told me his story. I was eager; he knew he had to speak very slowly for an Asian to understand his American English. I could follow him when he was speaking slowly to me.

He said he was a war veteran. He had his heyday. He had a family, a wife, children, and grandchildren. He served in the Vietnam War. I didn't understand the ranking, nor did I want to know what rank he held in the army. He had made his money, his family was well settled, but one day—he did not know why—he lost his erection. He consulted the best of doctors. He took a lot of medicines, but nothing helped. He had no erection.

Normally the wife does not like to get involved in any kind of sexual activity unless and until she receives her pound of flesh. Or she can use the guy to do things differently for her to achieve her orgasms. But in today's world, nobody has the patience, nor the mind, nor the time to allow the other person to be treated or understood in the proper perspective. A majority of people are like that. There are people who are great, nice, and willing to understand and support, but the majority has no time. They want the real one; they go to other places to find that pleasure or the solace. It's just a matter of the mind, training. Or maybe it's your karma or your faith or your destiny that takes you all the way.

This guy told me in short that he was told by a friend of his who used to go to Thailand regularly about the good times he had in Thailand. The amount of money spent in Thailand is very cheap compared to getting any kind of pleasures in the West. And people do say its dirt cheap to get all the services in Thailand depending on your knowledge on where to go to get the proper services. The guy said another war veteran had a problem, and his problem was solved after his regular visits to Thailand. So Thailand is the divine place where all your medical problems are tackled by doctors—by us, not qualified doctors, the Thai massage girls or the Thai massage ladies.

He decided to visit Thailand and told his family he's taking a holiday. They said, 'Go ahead and enjoy yourself.' There was no need to ask for permission from the family; he only had to tell them. In Asia, it's different; you have to explain and give reasons for going out of your nest. It's again the culture. It's again the background. It's again the circumstances you're brought up in.

So he went and stayed in Bangkok for a few days. He took a lot of massages, did a bit of sightseeing; it was his first trip. Then he decided to go to Pattaya for three weeks. His program was for one month in Thailand, then he wanted to go to other places in Asia. He would complete his tour in three months' time, then he would get back home. He had come all the way from US. It was his first day in Pattaya, and he had gone to our three-star joint instead of going to a five-star one because he was advised by his friend to do it in a mediocre place to suit his budget. So he luckily went to my shop, he saw me, he liked me, and now I was with him in his room.

He thanked me, and he said, 'I'm very pleased with your services. Can we have this for all the three weeks I'm here so that hopefully I'll recover from my ailment?'

I suggested to him, 'Why not go and meet a doctor in Thailand? They're experts.'

He laughed at me. 'We get everything done in our army hospital. We get the best of doctors, the best of research and technology. And the doctors have said, "If at all you get an erection, it will be a miracle and will be magic. Try your luck. Nothing is wrong with trying." Let's try it out. Going to a doctor is a waste of big money. I have no problem. I can pay you good money. Let me have your massage therapy.'

I said, 'Fine.'

Then he got up. He told me to dress. I put on my bra and T-shirt, wore my white coat, and took my tools of the trade. He paid me a good amount of money—what was normally paid for a sex session or an intercourse, two thousand baht. That was sixty or sixty-five US dollars.

I thanked him and said, 'Whenever you want me to come, I'm willing to come.'

He said, 'Fine, thank you very much.'

I said bye. I gave him a kiss on his cheek, and he reciprocated with a small hug. No sexuality involved in it; it was affection. I had received money from him. I was thankful to him. I said bye and departed.

I went back to the shop after the massage; all the girls were busy with their respective customers. The next day, all my friends were given the story by me, and I asked for their suggestions to help my customer to regain his erection. They all gave their own suggestions on how I should do the massage. There were many who were more experienced and many who were not experienced, but each one gave their ideas.

I said, 'I'll do my best.'

I consulted my boss, told her there was a customer who had a problem like this.

She said, 'You have to make him feel that he can do it. That guy has to build up that kind of positive vibe. I'm sure he must have been told all this by his psychologist, but from our side, you give him the confidence, and you continue to do whatever you're doing, which I think is the correct method.'

I said, 'Okay.'

I had consulted all these specialists in massage therapy. During the day, normal activity continued. Maybe it was four o'clock in the evening when there was a call to my cashier. She looked at me, and then I realized it must be my guy, the customer, the American. I was asked to go. It was for two hours. I got ready with my uniform, a white coat, and my kit with the oil and products for the massage. Then I went and knocked on his room. He smiled and called me inside. Then he removed his dress and lay down. So I started working on him.

He was relaxing. He told me that he went out in the morning, visited a few places in Pattaya. He went to Nong

Nooch Village, where there were a lot of elephants, plenty of flowers, and plenty of entertainment activity organized. He saw the dolphin show and other attractions available in Pattaya. Being a tourist, he did his circuit of seeing places.

Then I said, 'It's very nice.'

He asked me whether I had visited all this places, and I said yes. I told him I had done all this with my boyfriend.

'Oh, you have a boyfriend?'

I said, 'Yes.'

'Very good for you.'

I thanked him, and then I continued to work on him.

It is an intricate work to be done very slowly so that no nerves are overstrained or damaged. You have to do it slowly and correctly. It took me an hour or so to finish the normal massage, and then I was concentrating on his penis area. There was definite improvement, and there was a small erection. He was getting excited. He wanted to again touch me; I went through the ritual of removing my bra and shirt. He was stroking and touching my breasts, and there were vibrations in his penis. It went on for quite some time, then he stopped like yesterday, and then he was exhausted.

Maybe there can be a dry ejaculation. You don't need an erection. Let's say, in a normal big one, the semen has to come out. Here you can still feel complete if you're excited, and that's as good as if you have finished your masturbation or you've finished the act. Mentally, you get satisfied. It is nothing but a huge psychological issue. A guy gets excited by seeing porn, by seeing a beautiful lady, or by dreaming or fantasizing about a particular person. It's the stimuli which produce the erection. Sometimes even without an erection, you're excited, and you can go through the process and complete the whole act. It's the mind and the body which have to coordinate with each other.

A person can do anything or so many things for the sake of having sex. If you go through the history of humans, many kingdoms have been lost for the sake of a woman. Many wars have been fought for the sake of a woman. It's the whole meaning of birth and death. We may work hard to produce money, and for what? To have physical comforts—this is done for the sake of your family. Again the family concept was later introduced into the civilization. Earlier it was not there; anybody can have sex with anyone just like that. Later, there were the polygyny and polyandry systems.

Now polygamy is most popular in the world—one man with many women. In Arab countries or Muslim countries, there are certain rules and regulations. You can have up to four wives; that's polygyny. Polyandry is one woman having many husbands. There are many who do it; maybe not with the society's legal sanctions or not within the government's rules and regulations, but it does happen, a woman living with many. An example of a prostitute or a massage lady who gives a massage, who does a happy ending, who has sex with many men is no problem. Maybe it is a form of polyandry.

As long as men and women are there, there is bound to be such activities. There are bound to be all kinds of permutations and combinations of the same sex, like gay and lesbian (woman to woman) marriages. All this is part of life. All this has been there for a long time. Through the evolution of society on the dictates of many wise guys, a set of rules were all provided for husbands, wives, and children. One man and one lady produce children and bring them up, be happy and enjoy the society's goodies, and give back to the society. This is the story crafted for the well-being of humanity.

So my customer finished his rest after his dry run inside himself. He was happy. He got up, dressed, and thanked me. Meanwhile, I took care of myself; I put back my bra, T-shirt, and white coat and waited for him. He paid me the same amount as yesterday. He hugged me, and he said he'd call me back. I wished him all the best, thanked him, and left the room. So the second episode was good.

I was making two thousand baht without having to go through the process of having a sexual encounter with a stranger. From my heart, I didn't want it. I was very happy with my guy, who would come once in three months. Maybe for a lady who is forty years old, the urge gets reduced; if you have all the rest and all the money in the world, you may indulge, but not for a hard-working lady, who gets tired and looks forward to taking rests. That's how life goes on.

It became a regular affair—me going and massaging this man from America. He was slowly recovering. He felt maybe more rejuvenated. I suggested to him after a week of taking care of him that he should try another girl from my shop. A change of touch of a person and a different body, structure, face, colour, could be exciting to him. He may get a bigger erection than what he was getting, a very small one as of that day.

He asked me, 'You're going to lose your business.'

I said, 'There is no resentment. It is only that we are trying to help you with your problem. We will be more than happy if your problems will be solved. You should be happy in your life and enjoy whatever you're blessed with by the god.'

He was very appreciative, and he said, 'Fine. You send someone of your choice.'

I thanked him. I had already earned from him fourteen thousand baht. I went down and told the other five girls that this was what I said. They were all excited; maybe they were proud of me, or some thought I was a fool. I had let go of a source of money. Whatever they thought was no concern of mine. My aim was to make that guy good.

So I told each one of them my plan of action, 'Let's see, we have another two weeks before the guy goes back. We hope to help him out. Each one of you go on one day and then repeat. Give me a progress report.'

They all said, 'Fine.'

My cashier was laughing, and she said, 'Will I get a chance?'

I said, 'If you want to.'

She said, 'No, I don't know how to massage.' She was only an accountant; she was a very thin girl, plain-looking, good in accounts, and she was not interested in massage work.

So the first girl went; her report was encouraging. So all the five girls took two sessions, and ten days were completed. He had another four days left before his departure for his home. The guy had sent word that I should go to see him tomorrow.

I went back to him. And he said, 'I have another four days left. Why don't you do the massage for me? I like you.'

I said, 'It's fine, no problem.'

Then I took over, and I used all the meagre knowledge I had. He'd been treated by five different girls. I removed my dress totally. Women totally naked might not look very beautiful—that was a feeling expressed by many people I had met. Whatever it was, I kept my skin-coloured underwear to cover my vagina. He liked to touch my breasts. I went to him.

I told him, 'For a change, I will lay down. You come on me, and I shall work on you.'

So he followed my instructions. He squatted on his feet, and he came on top of me. He was almost near my breasts, and his tool, which was hanging, was touching my breasts. I told him to put it between my breasts, and I held both my breasts and started massaging him. There was a slight movement, then I slowly took it in my mouth, and I started sucking his penis slowly. There was always a movement, but there was no erection.

I kept on doing it for some time, and then he said, 'It is painful.' Then I let go and made him lie down, and I started again massaging him. Later, after one and a half hours, I took his penis in my hand, put on a lot of oil, and I started masturbating him. I kept on moving it up down, rotating, turning, using both hands to do a motion of not up and down but rotating it. I did everything possible; there was a slight improvement, and his eyes were glittering. I think he was feeling something, so I kept on doing it, and finally, he shouted, saying, 'I'm coming!'

Nothing came. Again I felt it must be a dry ejaculation; he must have felt it. This was a point many of my friends who were experts in this work had told me. Many men who are old can't get semen out. That's an issue, but they can get an ejaculation inside through that feeling that gives the man the required happiness; it's all in the mind.

He was very pleased. He said, 'Did anything come out?'

I said, 'No. No problem. It's gone in. Maybe it will come if you keep on trying.'

He profusely thanked me. He hugged me and kissed me on my cheeks, and then he went to the restroom and came back. He told me that when he passed urine, there was a slight stickiness.

Then I said, 'It must be your semen. You're getting ready for big action in time to come. Maybe when you go back home, you can go to your doctor with this experience. They may help you out, and you can be happy.'

He was very pleased with this. Then he told me to go near him; once again, he held me and gave me three thousand baht, a bonus. He had another three days left, and I continued to serve him. On the last day, before he left, he said, 'Come with me for dinner to your favourite place.' I took him to my usual Thai food restaurant and offered him to eat some nice fish and prawns, and he ordered a few things which were less spicy and more suitable to his taste.

Then we went back. He thanked me and said, 'Tomorrow I'm leaving. Thank you for everything. God bless. Maybe I'll come back with a total erection. Maybe I'll have a go with you.'

I said, 'It will be my pleasure. Come, no problem at all. If you get a good erection. That's a reward to me. It will be on the house.'

He just laughed, and he gave me a small gift. I opened it. When I got back to my room, there were five thousand baht.

People can be very good to you. We call people who gives us things good, and if they don't give us things, we call them bad. This is absolutely wrong. There are many whom we call good just because they understand the other person's point of view. Treat with respect a person who goes to this particular kind of surroundings for a reason, and respect that reason instead of treating them like dirt or treating them like a commodity or treating them as a thing to be used and thrown.

I'd had many customers who just treated me like dirt or with contempt after I finished my job with them. In the beginning, they were all sweet and honey-like; that was an experience I had gone through. I was sure any person in my trade had gone through many such situations.

My life was on its normal routine after the guy left for his country. He was a special customer, and that customer had brought me around twenty thousand baht as bonus, which went into my savings, the real savings, for whatever I was building up for my dreams of wanting many nice things in life.

Let's see, if Buddha will bless me and if Buddha will give me the opportunity to fulfil all my dreams, I'm confident that, through my hard work, my destiny will take me to a big place, and I will be somebody to reckon with. Every person has an ambition; we should work hard to score the goals to have a hat-trick.

Chapter 20

So the next year, the fourth year, more money came in, and my mind was getting more greedy. I wanted to settle down as I was already forty plus. I started thinking of other methods through which I could earn money. I wanted to buy land, more land. We had a very little area, and I wanted to buy another piece of land next to my land, which had come for sale.

I wanted money, and when my boyfriend came I told him, 'I need money to buy land. I can manage some of it. How much can you give me?'

He said he could give a little, but I wanted more than he could give. We had an argument, then he said, 'I can give what I can. I cannot give more than that because I have my own commitments.'

I was angry with him. I fought with him. For two days of his week's stay, we did not even hug each other. I assumed that I went beyond my limit, and he would not visit me again.

I was more frustrated. There were tears in my eyes. I could see his face was pale when he said bye to me with a small squeeze of my hands. I didn't know his emotions, but I could feel he was sad. I felt that I went out of control, and the damage was done.

I was not willing to keep quiet. I had to think of something else to make more money. So luckily or unluckily, my fate or my luck took me to experience a new phase of life.

We don't know why an incident takes place on which you have absolutely no control. We are led to it by an unknown guiding hand.

I met a customer, a very nice, fat man through a friend of mine. He was in the hospitality trade. I told him my problem. I told him I was looking for more money, and I needed to earn in a quick time. In Thailand, being a massage lady is a seasonal business. In rainy days, for nearly three to four months, the business is very lean. For the balance, the eight months, the business is good.

If I had work, I would get money. If there was no customer, I wouldn't get money. That was the case. I was in a mediocre joint, a middle-class joint, a three-star hotel. Then that man, a good man, suggested, 'Why don't you go to Malaysia? There's a lot of opportunities there to earn more money.' He explained to me that I could go any time. 'With it being a neighbouring country, you don't need a visa. You can go join a Thai outlet—there are many outlets of local guys with Thai partners—and make more money.'

I jumped at this opportunity. I went with another lady who was also like me, in need of more money, to work in the suburbs of Kuala Lumpur, the capital of Malaysia. With it being a Muslim country, my explanation at the immigration was that I was going to meet a boyfriend of mine. Jolly well, they might have known that I was going there to work, like scores of needy ones, but they were good Samaritans. They let me into their country, and I started working as a massage lady. I was making better money than I was earning in Thailand.

Malaysia has a combination of Vietnamese, Cambodians, Indonesians from Bali, and of course, the locals. There is a statutory ban for a Malaysian Muslim woman to work in this field. Being in a multicultural Muslim country, I suppose, we all had the opportunity to work, to earn money; that was how I started making money. I could stay only for a period of twenty-five days at a stretch; beyond that, it would be a problem. I would need a work permit for a longer stay.

I had to go back to the nearest city in Thailand after twenty-five days, stay for a week, and then go back to Malaysia. The same procedures, same customers, same massages, same happy endings, and of course, no sex, no intercourse, cameras, all these problems; my life was going on like that. After three months, my heart was aching for my boyfriend. I called him, and he spoke to me with the same fervour, the same feelings, the same affection.

He said, 'The number is different.'

I said, 'I'm in Malaysia.'

He was surprised and shocked. 'Why are you there?'

I said, 'I am working here, and I am fine.'

'Are you safe? Have you got a permit to work?' So many questions.

I said I had taken care of all that. Then he said he was coming next month to Thailand to visit me. I was overjoyed. I thought that our relationship was cut or finished because I had insisted on big money when he had said he would only give whatever he could.

I organized my twenty-five-day period of working in Malaysia. I went back to Thailand for a week. He came, and everything was fine. He gave me whatever he could. That was okay, and I was making more money in Malaysia. So the fifth year went on like that.

On the sixth year, again it was a similar situation. My ambition, hard work, and desire made me accumulate more money because of my Malaysian work and whatever my boyfriend was giving. My expenses were the same, but my savings became more. My old boss who had the shop in the three-star hotel where I was working earlier wanted to sell it. My boss was a good lady; she had a boyfriend from Hong Kong. Her weakness was gambling and drinking—more of gambling and less of drinking.

She had lost heavily in one of her gambling sprees and, being a brave lady, was ready to face the vagaries of life boldly. She offered to sell that shop in the market. I was tempted. I was interested, and I wanted to own the shop. Of course, it was a rental shop, and I'd have to pay rent to the hotel, electricity, water, air conditioning charges, maintenance, etc. After all that, I could make decent money from the earnings of the four or five girls who worked there. My boyfriend came, and we had a long discussion on the pros and cons of the investment and how to raise that kind of money. We both chipped in and took a loan, and then I purchased that shop where I had worked as a massage girl. I became the owner of that shop; it was a great feeling. My boss, whom I respected and appreciated, wished me all the best. Money changed hands, and I started earning money from that shop.

Through the shop's earnings, my earnings in Malaysia, and my boyfriend steadily giving what he could every three or four months when he visited me for a week or ten days, life became more interesting. In Malaysia, there are very many tourists. I have great respect for all of them. Though Malaysia is an Islamic country, they are also humans, and they also have needs. Tourists and locals, all were visiting massage shops to take away the stress and satisfy their urge to feel nice and happy. Whatever the religion you follow, when it comes to a female, the man is a man, and he wants the female body. The human body is made of those kinds of chemicals, and the man and woman are born out of sex energy; man and woman are both sex starved. I was told by my friend that a woman has eight times more sexuality than a man. I don't know; it is what I've heard. They say every part of a woman's body is sexual, starting from the eyes to the hair and to their feet. Man has only a few things.

So business was good. The only thing was that we were not supposed to work there. My boss was an influential person with good connections. Most of the massage shops were owned by influential people from all walks of life. One day, four of us—all Thai girls—were caught by the police. We had no work permit, so we were arrested and put in a jail for three days. It was very traumatic and frustrating. Fortunately for us, my boss was well connected. We got pizzas, burgers, and food to eat. And after three days, we were let off, and the boss took care of us and asked us to go home and come back again.

All the double standards, all the rules, all the regulations by the government—all these things are enforced by men and women. Everybody has feelings, everybody has wants, and everyone knows the needs. But in the East or in Asia, people understand why a lady or a man goes to another country all the way from their country obviously in search of money, just because they cannot make enough in their place to fulfill their needs. So they go to earn in a new place; that's what happens.

Anyway, I was lucky and grateful to Malaysia that I was able to make more money by giving my services. The worst part is, there are many girls who are all the time into the flesh trade only. For them, it is only sex, and they get worn out faster. We were at least in massage services, so our survival was better than those in the flesh trade.

Then my life in the sixth year, seventh year, and eighth year had the same routine of massages, happy endings, little sexual encounters, and my guy's visits. I was forty-three, getting older but looking young—no issue. People would say I was twenty, twenty-five before a massage or before a happy ending. The same person would say I was thirty, thirty-two after it was finished. The initial attraction would go away while the work was being done. Anyway, I was forty-three, but I looked like thirty, thirty-one—strong, healthy, and making more money.

Chapter 21

In KL (that's Kuala Lumpur), I served customers from all over the world, but most were Asians and particularly people from neighbouring countries. One such lady who came for an oil massage chose me to do the massage for her. She was beautiful, tall, and maybe forty years old. She took a liking to me and chose me to do an oil massage for two hours. I took her to the first floor, made her comfortable, told her to change, and then I came with my oil and started the massage.

She had a beautiful body, well curved, absolutely stunning. I kept on working on her; she was enjoying the massage. She asked me, 'Where are you from?'

I knew she knew where I was from, but still she had asked me a question, so I had to answer her back. 'I'm from Thailand, ma'am.'

'Oh, you're from Thailand. Nice.'

Then we were chit-chatting generally, and she said she was a mistress of a very rich man. She had come for a holiday. She had all her people in the hotel nearby, and she went out to have a massage.

I said, 'Ma'am, they have a massage shop in the hotel.'

'Yes, I know. I wanted to go out and not be in that surroundings.'

I said, 'Thank you for your business, ma'am.'

She said, 'You are welcome.'

Then I finished her back portion, and she turned. She lay down on her back, and she was looking at me. Now that I'd been in the massage work for a long time, I felt with my experience that she was hungry for sex. I kept on massaging her on her well-formed, firm breasts. I had to do it; it was part of the job. Her nipples became swollen, her breasts were swelling, and she was moaning soundlessly. It was her dignity. She told me through sign language, by holding my hand, to continue doing it.

I said, 'Yes, ma'am.' I kept on working on her breasts. I had massaged many women, many girls, and many young and old. It was purely a mechanical movement and the right pressure on the right places. We avoided certain areas— let's call those the sex zones. We did touch the breasts, the nipples, just a moment of slight flattening from all the four sides. And then we would go down, and it would be the same. We didn't go to the vaginal part. We would do it up to the small stomach and to the thighs and go down.

Then she said to me, 'You're good.'

And I said, 'Thank you.'

And she asked me to rotate her breasts and press them a little hard, and then she asked me to touch her anal–vaginal portion.

I said, 'Madam—'

She said, 'Don't say anything. Just do what I say.'

She took out, believe me, big money—one thousand ringgits from her purse kept near her; it was a lot of money. She put it in my hand, and she told me to take care of her vagina with one hand and the other hand on her breasts; she herself was touching herself in different places. I looked at the other partitions; luckily, there were no customers. I said, *What the heck! I will help her out with whatever she wants me to do.*

It took quite some time. She was a hell of a strong woman with plenty of passion. I finished what she wanted, and I think she had a big orgasm. She was totally spent, happy, relaxed. She got up, hugged me, kissed me on my cheeks, and then she requested me to kiss her on the lips. I had never done it. I did it because she was like a desperate child wanting something. It comes from inside, I suppose, and when people want something and they don't get it, they'll do anything to achieve it.

This lady was very pleased. She got herself ready. She asked me for some hot tea, which I happily gave her. Then she said she'd come tomorrow, and I said, 'You're welcome, madam.' Then we went down to the ground floor, and she paid the bill for the massage. She gave me a tip of one thousand ringgits (that's Malaysian currency). It was equivalent to three hundred US dollars. The cashier and the other girls' eyes were all popping out. So much tip.

I said, 'She's a nice lady.'

And everybody said, 'Good, you are lucky today.'

I was confused. I told the cashier I would go eat something and come back. She said, 'You're hungry? Go. No problem.' Then I went out to a shop nearby. I bought a soft drink, which I knew was not good for my health, but I needed something to drink. So I finished my drink and sat in confusion. I was wondering I have heard, I have not seen; it was an open acceptance by a person who is in need.

Generally, women control their emotions. There are many who gratify themselves, but it needs money, courage, and boldness to ask for a favour in a strange place, especially for an Asian woman. Maybe in the West there are designated places where you can get whatever you want, but it's not so for a female in Asia, especially in Malaysia. In Thailand, yes, there's that possibility, which was something I had not encountered so far.

I was heavy-headed. I had to admit that in the process of making that lady happy and giving her that happy ending, I myself had an orgasm without anybody touching me, without anybody making me feel physically. It was a mental feeling. It was like a wet dream for a man; for any man, his fantasies and dreams bring out a wet dream for him. Similarly, women can also get an orgasm by dreaming on certain things and if the intensity is of a very high level.

I was forty-three years old. I had seen so much sexual activity with my customers and with my boyfriend, but this was my first encounter where I had an orgasm without being touched anywhere. Maybe my touching or giving an orgasm to that lady must have triggered my orgasm.

The next day, I subconsciously wore a better dress. I made myself up to look more beautiful, I suppose. Then I went to the shop a little earlier than the usual because I never wanted to miss out. It was big money she gave me the day before. She did not come at four o'clock as yesterday. It became five o'clock, and my turn might come. Of course, if she came after I had gone to another customer, either she would have to wait for me if she wants me or she could take somebody else. But a customer came, and it was my turn. I had to take the person; it was a man who wanted a foot massage, and that was done in the ground floor. So I was thankful to my god. Still I could see if she came.

So then I started working with this man on his foot. I was halfway through when the lady entered. She smiled at me, and I smiled at her. Then she told the cashier she wanted me for an oil massage. Then the cashier said, 'There are many other girls. You can choose any one of them.' She pointed at me and said she wanted me. Then the cashier said, 'You have to wait or come back after half an hour.' She said, 'No problem.' She sat down in the waiting area and started reading a magazine; she was educated, good-looking, and sophisticated. They offered her some tea, but she refused. I was fast in completing my massage. I couldn't reduce the time; I had to do one hour. The clock was set, and it was a discipline to be followed. I finished my massage with that man, and he thanked me. I went out to wash my hands and put on some cologne to smell good. Then the guy gave me a tip, and I opened the door for him to leave.

Once I finished with him, I called the lady, 'Let's go up.' And she said, 'Fine.'

Then we climbed the stairs up to the first floor. She went in, and she hugged me. I didn't hug her back, only a small movement with my hands. Then I gave her a towel; she changed and lay down on the bed. She asked me to sit next to her; I sat next to her.

She started touching me. Then she said, 'My dear, don't worry. I won't eat you up or do anything wrong.' I kept quiet; then after some time, she told me, 'You do the massage.'

I said, 'Thank you, ma'am.' Then I worked on her expertly, quickly, fast, and strongly as she was tired; she said she had a hard day. She went out with the family to shop; she walked, walked, and walked, and it was good that she took some rest when I was with that man, doing the foot massage. Then after one hour or so, I completed the basic massage, then she was on her back and asked me to work on her with little variations. Human nature is such that we want many varieties.

Then she took out from her purse an artificial dildo, and she asked me to use it with my hand. I had no choice, but I took it upon myself to do what my boyfriend used to do to me with his original tool. She was totally getting excited, and she had a very big orgasm. She was totally spent; she was controlling her outbursts, being a very dignified and educated lady. Emotions can become outbursts. She shouted once. I told her, 'Slowly, slowly.' Then she controlled herself. She hugged me. She held me for some time, and then she settled down.

She changed and said she was leaving that day, back to her place, her prison, where her husband had no time nor the capacity to make her happy. 'I'm resigned to my fate and my destiny, and it's only when I come out like this that I try to find some solace.' I thanked her for the nice words she said to me, and she said, 'No problem.' And she gave me double the money. I wasn't surprised because for her money wasn't an issue. And she said, 'Be good, be happy. When I come next time, I'll definitely come to your place.' I thanked her profusely. Then she left.

My luck was changing; there were sporadic opportunities like that wherein I would get big money. We don't know who the accountant is who gives and takes from us. Sometimes you never save; money never gets accumulated. Sometimes you keep on saving, that is how I own a massage shop, and that extra land income. Now I was hoping to do more activities to earn money. I had plans to go to Korea. I was totally confused. I was not sure of what I should do. I said I'd do it easy and cool instead of rushing and losing whatever I had. So things were moving on this basis.

Sometimes I would get very bad customers in KL. It was normal—only Thai massage and oil massage. There are a lot of rules and police problems as far as this industry is concerned. It's like they want the tourists, and the tourists want something; they want to give it, but at the same time, they don't want to give it. Of course, the local girls are not enough to cater to the needs of the tourists. There are a lot of Thais, a lot of Filipinos, Malaysians, and of course, there are Indonesians mainly from Bali. That's how this particular trade survives. The body needs relaxation. Once relaxation comes in, it needs more. That's how the whole system is created.

I was wondering about that lady who had everything—all the money, all the beauty—but there was no one to love her. Why wouldn't she find a nice lover who could really satisfy her and make her happy? Then I suddenly realized that the lady had left her dildo. I rushed upstairs—of course, not with great haste so that the other girls wouldn't get suspicious. Luckily, the bed in the area where I had worked on the lady was untouched, and I had put the dildo on the side. I took it, put it in a plastic bag, wrapped it, and threw it into a dust bin. That was it. I didn't need it because I was not interested in it.

People have so many needs, so many diversities, so many wishes, and all can't be fulfilled. You have something, and then you don't have the other thing. Only this other thing can get you this something. It's rare to find a person with everything. You always see a lady or a family who has two sons or three sons or four sons or only sons. There are many families with only daughters and daughters. They want a boy, but they can't get it. They want a girl, but they can't get it. As I said, there is somebody who keeps tabs on all of us. So it is all set, and destiny has its mysterious ways. Instead of cursing the power or the universe, the godliness or the god, we should have patience and wait for the universe to deliver whatever we are eligible to get. It's a great philosophy, but nobody has the patience or time or the mind to wait;

everybody wants to grab what they can. That's where all the misery and problems start.

We had a Thai man as a customer. All the three girls from Thailand who worked in our shop were excited to see a Thai man. He was quite handsome, good-looking, smiling, and must be an executive with some company. He came, and it was his choice to choose from many. We three were there, and there were some Balinese girls and Malay girls to choose from. He selected me, and he wanted an oil massage. Generally, it was all the men who needed a bit of relaxation, and oil massage was the best. The whole body would get rejuvenated by the proper movement of the hands, easing the strain of all the nerves in the body.

So this guy went into the room. I gave him a towel. He changed and lay down on his back; he knew the procedure. I started working on him expertly and professionally. We shared a common border, road transport between Thailand and Malaysia. He was quiet. I was quiet. It was normally the practice; we didn't speak unnecessarily, and we would just say, 'You want it strong, soft? Any pain? You want any special attention?' I massaged him for half an hour or so. It was a one-hour massage. I then made him turn on the other side.

He started talking. Maybe he was not comfortable talking without seeing the face of the person; there are many like that. He said 'You're from where?' and 'How are you working here?' and all that—the normal small talk. I politely replied to him.

I asked him, 'You're on business or you're a tourist?'

'No, I came here on business.' Then he said, 'You're a good massage lady.'

I said, 'Thank you.'

'You make more money here than in Thailand'.

I said yes. Then the ultimate question: whether he could have a happy ending.

I said, 'No, it's not allowed in this shop.'

Then he said, 'We both are Thais. You can come to my hotel room.'

I said, 'That is possible after my working hours, which end at one o'clock, after midnight.'

Then he said, 'Okay. I'm here for three or four days. What are your working hours?'

I said, 'We start at around three o'clock in the afternoon and go on to about one o'clock, which is the closing time. But there are customers, it can be at two o'clock, three o'clock in the early morning.'

Then he said, 'Is it possible that we can meet at your free time?'

I said, 'I'll go back to my room, sleep for six hours, and get ready. I can come by twelve o'clock.

He said, 'Fine.' He gave me his number and told me to call him whenever I was ready the next day, and he said he'd adjust his timings. He told me he'd come and take me. It's dangerous to go out with strangers but it's always an adventure; I'd always wanted to try. Then he said on his own, 'Money is not a problem. I'll pay you good.' I said okay.

Still I trusted people, and of course, I had nothing to lose. Of course, my efforts was the one I might lose if I did not get paid properly. Then he came around twelve o'clock the next day near our massage shop. I normally didn't take risks in going anywhere else in KL because the authorities might ask me, cops could ask me any time for my work permit. If they saw me on the street, I could always say I was a tourist. But in the shop, I would need a work permit. But still they could ask me for my papers.

He came in a taxi, came out, shook hands with me, and said, 'Sawadee khap.' In Thai, that is 'How are you?' He took me in the car. We both were Thais, so we made the perfect couple. So he took me to his room. Then he wanted to immediately have a go. I said, 'Wait, don't be in a hurry.' Then I changed, and he started getting ready. He started kissing me and holding me. I told him, 'You have a condom?' Then he said, 'I thought you must be carrying one.' I just told him I was not in the profession of giving sex. I was in the profession of giving a massage. Then he said, 'Wait, I will go and get it.' Then he just went out to the drug store, bought some condoms, and came back.

Then he started touching me. All his pent-up emotions, he was putting them out. My body was reacting, but my mind was not reacting. I had a bit of reservations. I wouldn't call it psychological; maybe my mind was prejudiced in being with a Thai man after my husband left me. Believe me, I never had an affair, or what you would call a sexual affair, in the massage business with a Thai man. It was the first after my ex-husband. There had been Europeans and other Asians with whom I had sex with for the sake of money. But this time, it was with a Thai man. I went through the process mechanically. I faked a big orgasm for him. Of course, my body had reacted, and there was a small orgasm.

That is the reason it is said that this body is made out of bones, blood, water, flesh, muscles, and all the chemicals which in turn produce that kind of result when you go through the process. That is the reason there are many women who are called frigid; they don't react because deep down they have pain somewhere in their minds and they fail to react. I'm not a frigid woman. I'm a lovely and lively woman. But this encounter with a Thai man was not very palatable. Of course, we had to digest all things, even those we don't like. You have to pretend you do like it. I think it is the way the power has made us, and we have to go through the process.

He was very happy, and I showed my enthusiasm; it was a fake one (sorry). He felt he had his fill of pleasures, and he said, 'Fantastic, you're very nice.'

I said, 'Thank you.'

He asked me, 'Would you like to stay longer?'

I said, 'No, it's already time for me to go get ready and go to the shop.'

He said, 'Okay.' He also had to catch up with his work. Then he paid me three thousand baht; that was equivalent to one hundred US dollars. That was good money, and he told me he would drop me off.

I said, 'Don't bother.' I took my purse, bid him farewell, and returned to my room. I took hot and cold showers and kept applying a lot of soap all over me. I was not happy, just feeling a little sad. Maybe this guy had reminded me of my husband and all the good times I had with him and the family. I had two children with him. And that guy, just like that, left me for another woman. It was shattering. My ego was hurt. What was not there in me that was there in that other woman? Maybe I was a little cocky, or I had answered him back and was more vocal with my demands. As I have been saying time and again, men want slaves or men want 'Yes, sir' women so they can have their ways with them and exploit them.

Chapter 22

I was strong, healthy, good-looking, beautiful, radiant. Now I knew how to put on make-up. There are so many age-reducing creams which the multinationals thrust upon us. To become white and have baby skin, we use a lot of baby products to become like a baby. What a mirage. What a thought. Today, cosmetics companies make millions out of all these gullible people like me and others. We want to look beautiful; that's the only thing. So we're willing to spend any amount of money for that. It is said beauty is skin-deep and transient and that beauty is temporary. All of us will become old one day, and nobody will notice us. Everybody wants to look great, nice—if not for the customers, then for their husbands or boyfriends.

My family was very happy. I forgot to tell you that my first son fell in love with a girl, had a sexual relationship with her, and produced a baby, which was delivered prematurely; it was put in an incubator. The child survived, and later we came to know that the girl was from a nearby village. Then I met the parents of the girl, and they both got married; now I have two grandsons. My tragedy in Thailand struck my son also. But it was different. His wife left him, and the two children of theirs are taken care of by the parents of the girl. They are financially sound, still I pay a good amount every month for the upkeep of my two grandchildren, on behalf of my son.

My son was working as a helper in some factory. I wouldn't call him a liability. All children are our pleasure, but the fact remained that I had to take care of him on certain issues. It's said in Buddhism that it's a great merit for a son to become a monk for a short period of twenty-one days, fifteen days, or so. My son wanted to go after she left him, so I spent quite a lot of money. He shaved his head, wore the monk robe, and fed the monks and the community. We all carry out the traditions, customs, and responsibilities created by our forefathers. So this is the story of my first son.

My second son was now seventeen; he played football. In Thailand, the passion is football. He needed good shoes; football shoes cost big money—Nike, Adidas, so many brands. I took care of him now that I had the money. I had my shop money, my work money, and a little help from my boyfriend. And of course, my first son brought in little money, but that was spent for his own expenses, and he gave that to his grandmother in the village, where he lived now.

I was beautiful—that was what everyone said. I knew how to look well. I took care of my body. Now I was forty-three. Maybe in another seven years or less, I could still work as a massage lady. I understood what would happen to me when I became fifty. Nobody would want an old lady to massage them. I would tell this to most of the girls whom I met who were in a similar trade: 'Save, take care, have money for your future and for your old age.' Many would listen; many didn't. Then it would be their fate, karma, or destiny. Lord Buddha will take care of all of us. This was what the monks said, and I very strongly believed in it.

Recently, for a week I became a nun. Of course, a lady didn't have to shave her head unless she became a permanent nun. We wore white robes. We got up in the early morning, at five o'clock, and cleaned the bathrooms, toilets, and the temple. Then we went to pray, and then we had a meal, which the temple provided. The whole day, we spent it listening, chanting, and repeating mantras or hymns, praising the Lord Buddha. I forgot the money angle, and the family worries for a week. I did it for a week, and honestly, I felt happy about it. I intended to do it many more times whenever I would find the time. I was a busy lady. I had commitments.

I developed a friends circle in Malaysia. These friendships stemmed from my good nature, from my own beauty, from my approach. There is a saying that civility costs nothing but can buy everything. You have to be nice to people, not be cocky, and not feel that you are very beautiful. No, it's not beauty and the beast; beauty and the beast can be tamed.

What is the mystery for all these complex situations in this world? No one knows. No one can explain. Man has developed so many technologies, so many things, and so many experiments, like going to the Moon and Mars. We have to accept that there is a power which produced all of us; it's more powerful than the human brain. Humans have produced many gadgets for their comfort. All gods are the creations of human beings. Some intelligent ones have cleverly introduced them to all of us. But we do find solace, peace, happiness when we visit a wat, temple, church, mosque, synagogue, any place of worship of any religion, or any beautiful landscape which represents nature. A lovely scenery in a village is so peaceful than the chaotic traffic in any urban area.

Chapter 23

I was happy in my own way. I was pleased with what happened to me after my boyfriend's visit to my village. I was getting more affection and love from my friends, relatives, and other members of the village. My ex-husband, who used to visit his sons once in a while, got the news and went for a quicker visit this time. He was hoping my second son would join the police or army. In Thailand when a boy reaches eighteen, his name is written on a piece of paper along with others of the same age, and it was put in a bowl in a Buddhist temple or in the army's recruiting centre. A monk picks up the paper, and the selected person goes for three years to work in the army, navy, or air force, or he can always choose to be a monk. My ex-husband hoped that my son would join the police or army so that he would get all the benefits from the government because he is the father and he has donated his sperm. I, their mother, had taken care of my children all these years, but he was not bothered about that. He was happy with his other wife, and the daughter of that lady.

Suddenly, he was interested. He would go to our village and give money to his sons once in a month. He wanted to assert his paternity rights on his children. He was also perturbed by my boyfriend's visit to the village. The good part was that, after saving some money, my friend who helped me go to Malaysia suggested that I buy a van or transport vehicle, which could fetch me a good amount of money monthly if I leased it out to the travel business which he ran. He got me a loan. I managed to get some money from my massage shop, and I bought a van, which fetched me an additional income apart from my shop and my work in Malaysia. I did not expect my boyfriend to give me any money. Of course, he steadily gave me whatever he could whenever he visited me once in five months, six months. My ex-husband, who came to know that I had bought a van, owned a shop, had a boyfriend, worked in Malaysia, and had four sources of income, was trying to be nice to me, and I did not even want to look at his bloody face. I hated him! He was the father of my children—okay, fine—but now he came to me and said that we were not properly divorced and that he had slogged for the family for so many years. He asked me—can you believe it—to give him a good amount to sign the papers for our divorce. He promised to give me a lot of trouble if I did not comply.

All the neighbours, all the relatives tried to make him understand. 'The lady makes money by working hard. Sometimes she works for the whole night. Customers come—drunk customers, drug-addicted customers. But any customer is a customer, so she has to serve them.' From such a person, my ex-husband was demanding money for release from the marriage which he committed to dissolve in front of all the elders. He claimed certain things, and I was supposed to find the money to settle his account once and for all so that we could get a proper divorce. Even after I'd get the divorce, he would continue to be my children's father. If they worked in a government office, army, or police, he would be entitled to the father's benefits. Most of the time, men make their wives earn money; they drink, enjoy, and go to other women. As I said earlier, a woman is the greatest enemy of a woman.

Now I intend to settle his account. I am forty-three and still have my boyfriend visiting me once in a while. Believe me, I'm greedy, and I feel that my time in Malaysia is running out. We always have that police problem.

I want quick money, and I'm already considered old by the standards of my business of massage work. I can be active until fifty, subject to my health being good. I was scared once, when my hand started feeling terribly painful, and I took a fifteen day rest.

Now it is okay. I have taken care of that problem. Now I'm thinking of going to South Korea. I believe I can get more money there. It is always no money, little money, little more money, more money. I can work for two, three years maybe— whatever the time I'm allowed to stay in South Korea. I don't know. Somebody has promised to take me there, a Thai lady. We are exposed to vagaries in an unknown place, unknown people, unknown language, universal language of the body, universal language of my hand working on the body of a human. Thank the god it is not a real beast, my hand. It was said by a dear friend of mine that when a man's tool (penis) is held in my hand for a happy ending, that guy will say, 'My future is in your hands.' Because of that, I am living. If men were not endowed with it, I suppose—I don't know—I would have to find a different job. Maybe I'd have to wash dishes or clothes in somebody's house to make a living for that extra money. Why so much disparity, problems? Why so much difficulties?

Anyway, that is it. Now I intend to go away.

My friend agreed, 'Okay, you go make your money. One year, two years, three years—it is up to you if you can withstand the pressure. Whenever you feel like it, you can come back.'

I'm at peace with him. My family has no problems with my decision; they are not bothered where I go, what I do as long as every month, I send them that money, that extra money, that emergency money required by them. Of course, they love me and want me to be happy, but the primary importance is the money which I am supposed to send them. My shop gives me a little money. I have employed five people. I am an entrepreneur. I am the boss of the shop. I am a worker in a massage shop in Malaysia. I have a van which produces money for me every month, thanks to my friend in Bangkok.

I thank my boyfriend for his support. I think he is my soulmate. He is of another nationality. What brought him here? What made me meet him? It has been nine years now, and he's a good man. God bless him. He loves me. I love the story of *Pretty Woman*, and the movie was great. I appreciate the great acting talents of Richard Gere and Julia Roberts.

Now I do not know what life holds for me. Will I continue to work in Malaysia, or will I go to Korea? I do not know. As of today, this has been my story; it is from my heart. Wherever you are in this world, in whichever country, please see to it that you help the poor, those in my kind of work. Treat them with love, compassion, and kindness. They're also human beings. You have more green bucks. You cannot take anything with you when you die. Care, share, love, be affectionate. Let them get at least one meal or all three meals. Let them also drink the Scotch you drink once in a while. Let them eat good food, the caviar, the seven-course dinners.

About the Author

Natesan Sarvanam has been a sales executive, banker, secretary to an aristocratic family, property developer, and deputy district governor for the Lions Club. He is a firm believer in equal rights and opportunities for women and girls. An avid traveller, he currently lives in Bangalore, Karnataka, India.

Printed in the United States
By Bookmasters